# SHOT THROUGH THE HEART

## MAREN BIRK

First Edition: February 2019
Website: www.MarenBirk.com
E-book Edition ISBN-13: 978-0-578-46587-6
Print Edition ISBN-13: 978-0-578-45184-8

❀ Created with Vellum

*For Heather*

# ACKNOWLEDGMENTS

My copyeditor, Jessica Snyder, thank you for assisting me with this project. I can't wait to work with you again.

Thank you to my wonderful writer friends: Brandy and Jane. I couldn't have done this without your encouragement and friendship. I'm so thankful to have both of you in my life.

To my friends: Pam, Stacey, Mo, Julia, and Lori. Thank you for reading, and re-reading. You all rock!

And to my biggest cheerleader, my mother, Deb. Thank you!

# CHAPTER ONE

"Line is hot, line is hot," yelled the Range Officer.

Aurora Cross hurriedly shoved a magazine into her Glock and took her stance. Heart pumping, she waited for the next words from the RO, Henry. "Shooter ready?"

She nodded her head, causing her long ponytail to swing, and called out above the din, "Ready."

Henry shouted, "Stand by!"

All thought left her as she focused on hitting the six metal plates eleven yards away. She forgot about the current problems at her job and worry over her dad.

*Aim, squeeze, repeat.* She aimed at the first plate and barely registered the recoil of the Glock. Sweat trickled down her back as she concentrated on the second plate and remembered to breathe. She didn't waste valuable time watching the plates go down after she hit them. Instead, she relied on the sound of bullets hitting metal and moved on to the next target. After hearing the pinging sound on the last plate, Rori tilted the gun to the side and removed the magazine. She pulled off her safety glasses and hearing protection, then adjusted her black cap down over her eyes.

Henry walked over and showed her the display on the shot timer, which presented a great time for her run. Pleased she had beaten her own time for this course and would probably place first in this Glock Sport Shooting Foundation match, she inwardly grinned. *At least something is going right in my life.* As she bent to bag up her pistol and empty magazines, two small-booted feet appeared in her line of vision.

*Crap.*

Did she really have to deal with Dwayne Tealy today? After he caused her one-week suspension from work, she couldn't stomach even looking at him. She should have realized he couldn't allow one shooting competition to go by without him trying to jump her, literally.

Rising to her full height of five foot seven, she glared into her nemesis's eyes. She was as tall as Dwayne, could out shoot him, and could probably take him down in a fist fight. She resisted the urge to roll her eyes at him, and bleakly dreaded the possibility of an impending argument. Especially after the last stint of trouble he had caused her. Her co-worker, and fellow police officer, looked like a weasel with beady little eyes and blah brown hair. *Be civil. You are a professional.*

Tossing her range bag over her shoulder, she stepped out of the shade the small canopy provided and gave him a terse nod. "Afternoon, Dwayne."

Walking around him was the plan, but the jerk reached out

and snaked his fingers around her arm, stopping her. Disgust filled her as she recalled the not too distant memory of his unwanted hands on another part of her body. She smelled his pungent aftershave, the same overwhelming scent that had coated her almost a month ago. She had showered repeatedly but couldn't remove his stench on her skin for days after.

"Rori, Rori…can't you talk to your old partner for a few minutes?"

*This is crap.* They had been partners for all of two seconds before her dad had stepped in and changed the chief's mind. Then Tealy had assaulted her. Not willing to go down that path today, she steadied herself. Jerking her arm free, she blew out the breath she had been holding.

"What do you want?" As far as she could tell, he wanted the same thing he always wanted—something that wasn't for sale.

Dwayne smirked. "Such a little firecracker."

"Just because your family is the richest in this town doesn't mean you can manhandle any woman in your proximity. Remember the ruling, you and I aren't to work together at all."

"But this isn't work. Rori, I like that you're so hot. All the time. Just imagine what it would be like between us."

She hitched her range bag higher on her shoulder with one hand while her other hand clenched into a fist. *Don't hit him again.* "It'll never happen. You disgust me. Move out of my way."

He had always gotten everything he had ever wanted—women, cars, and even jobs. His family's money had bought his way through the police academy. There was one thing his money hadn't been able to buy—her.

All through the academy, he had been the fly in her oint-
ment. If it hadn't been for her dad's long friendship with the
chief, Dwayne would have been her partner permanently.

A group of fellow officers had started to gather around the
canopy out of concern for her, but he wouldn't care. He knew
their co-workers wouldn't defend her for fear of being
suspended without pay as she had recently. He was above the
other officers at the range due to his father's connections. They
knew it, and he knew it. He would never be punished for "mess-
ing" with Rori.

She had asked her co-workers to stay out of the way, especially after the last time she and Dwayne had gotten into it. She
didn't want the loss of their jobs on her conscience and she
could take care of herself. The last incident over a month ago
clearly reminded her of the Tealys' status in this town. Wasn't
that what this place was about? Your family's status? Family
history decided one's fate…and Rori's fate had been determined
the moment her mom passed away.

"What do you want?"

"A dinner date? After dinner, we can go back to my place
for a nightcap." He grinned, and then had the audacity to wink.

Sickened by him, she held her stance. "You'd be better off
going home with your blow-up Suzy doll, 'cause that's the only
woman you'll be having dinner with tonight." Snickers ensued,
and she couldn't help the smile that broke out across her face.
Her co-workers couldn't defend her for fear of possible suspension or worse, but at least they laughed at her come-backs.

Hearing the laughter at his unsuccessful request, he sneered,
"You and your daddy think you are so much better than me,

don't you? Getting off with a one-week suspension when you should have been fired."

*Here we go again.*

"Yes, Dwayne, we are better than you, but you seem to keep forgetting it. Honest people are always better than lying perverts. Stop harassing me and get over yourself."

He lunged for her then, but she dodged to the side. Down he went. Face first, right in the gravel and dirt of the range. He lay on the ground for a few moments before rolling over and sitting up.

Resisting the urge to kick him while he lay in the dirt was difficult, but she couldn't afford another week without pay. She didn't want to dip into her savings, and she refused to ask her father for help. She could only hope this episode would last Dwayne at least a month before he tried to touch her again.

Squaring her shoulders, she tipped her head to the crowd watching her latest drama and walked on. The ATV carrying the first-aid supplies slowly made its way over to Dwayne. Bummer for him, but it looked like he was going to have some bruises. It wouldn't hurt his looks, as he had none.

As the crowd watched, he protested—loudly—his voice an octave higher. "She attacked me, just like last time. Did you see her? Crazy bitch."

Henry spoke up. "Now, Dwayne, just cut it out. Everyone here saw you trip on your own clumsy feet."

Rori stopped at Henry and whispered, "Shush, he isn't worth it." As she passed the rest of them, she muttered, "Have a good one, boys." Angry as she was with her co-workers, she didn't blame them for their lack of action. These men were honest, hard-working, family men. None of them could afford to lose their jobs. Even with her father's connections on the force, she was a prime example that Dwayne Tealy could cause trouble for all of them. His rich father supplied most of the jobs in the county, and his mother was the mayor. Yes, Dwayne was the golden boy of New Brick.

He could do whatever he wanted to her and nothing would ever be done about it. Sure, it was an impossible situation she didn't deserve, but moving wasn't an option, and neither was a new job. The force was part of her family's past, and she needed to keep the tradition going. She was an only child, and her dad was the last in a long line of Cross men who had served. She was the only one left to carry on the tradition, and with her mom's passing, she had lost her biggest cheerleader.

"Miss Cross?"

What the heck? Was she ever going to make it out of here? She just wanted to get home, take a cool shower, and enjoy a glass of wine.

The man repeated, "Miss Cross?"

"Who wants to know?" Leery of anyone calling her "Miss," she craned her neck to look at the dark-haired man before her—a tall, good-looking man. From her vantage point, she could also make out piercing gray eyes that made her stomach do a flip-flop. He reminded her of Josh Duhamel with his glorious dark hair.

The man held out his right hand while pushing his beat-up, brown leather messenger bag over his left shoulder. "My name is Guy Matthews, editor-in-chief of *Stock and Guns* magazine."

She shook his hand then whistled, "Wow. What is the editor of SG magazine doing here in Ohio?"

Mr. Tall, Dark, and Handsome laughed. "So, you have heard of us?"

"Yeah, you could say that. While other teenage girls were reading *Seventeen,* I was reading *Stock and Guns* and any other ammo magazines I could get my hands on."

"Well, Miss Cross, today is your lucky day. We have been following your shooting scores for a while, and your *Gun Girl* blog, and wanted to discuss a sponsorship opportunity with you."

"First off, let me be the judge of whether or not this is my lucky day. Second, who is this 'we' you've mentioned? I only see one of you. Third, call me Rori." She almost laughed at his shocked expression. Being the only woman on the police force, she treated most folks she met with the same attitude her co-workers received. It was hard to turn off, even with strangers.

He recovered quickly, "The 'we' is the board of *Stock and Guns*."

He smiled down at her, not at all bothered by her attitude. His broad smile revealed very white and straight teeth. This made her bristle up even more. He was a nice guy.

*Crap.* She loved a good smile, but she didn't want to appear too eager. "Well, Guy, talk to me while I walk to my car. I have an appointment." *With a cool shower and a glass of White Zin...*

She kept walking as he kept talking. Of course, she would meet the most handsome man she had ever seen while sweat dripped down her back and she was roasting in the July sun. Oh well, she really wasn't the girly type. She kept her blond hair pulled back in a ponytail, rarely wore make-up, and she was certain the sunscreen/bug screen she'd applied when she'd arrived at the range had canceled out the scent of her coconut body wash.

Tall, Dark and Handsome still talked, "…travel all over the country…" *Yada, yada.* Only half listening, she couldn't help but think today wasn't the day to listen to an important sales pitch. And Guy wasn't the best salesman.

She guessed he was a man used to calling the shots from a massive desk and letting others set things up for him. Dressed for a day on the range in khakis and a blue polo shirt, she imagined him in a suit instead. The man would fill out a suit nicely. She wondered if he could even shoot, or if he just stayed behind a computer all day. Or maybe he did both like her dad.

"Do you shoot, Mr. Matthews?"

He stopped at her abrupt question and answered a bit tersely, "Of course. What kind of editor of a gun magazine would I be if I didn't know how to shoot?"

"Do you hunt?"

"Yes, of course. Do you?"

"Hunting is a passion of mine. My father dragged me out into a blind at a young age."

"Good. Now, we have the important questions out of the way, would you like to hear more about my offer?"

"Mr. Matthews, I'm sure this is a great offer, and I would like to hear more…but I have a lot going on today." Picturing her dad, Rori realized she shouldn't be talking to Guy Matthews or contemplating any offers for a magazine deal involving travel. For some reason, though, she couldn't give him an outright refusal.

She stopped dead in her tracks. "Mr. Matthews, I'm sorry, but let me think about this a bit more."

\* \* \*

At her unexpected stop, Guy forgot his sales pitch. He was in awe of Aurora Cross. Skills alone had him crawling to her door, begging her to sign a sponsorship contract with his magazine. Her kiss-my-ass attitude, her looks, and the way she handled herself made her the ultimate package. He'd been determined to sign her based on the number of GSSF matches she had won, but now he was prepared to do anything to sign her. With Rori on his team, the National Magazine Award he had coveted for years would be within his grasp.

Thinking quickly, he pulled out all the stops as they walked to her bright red pickup. He wasn't surprised she drove a truck. She also didn't carry a big, girly bag. In fact, she was currently pulling her truck keys out of a hidden pocket in her camouflage shorts, while tossing her black range bag in the bed of her truck.

It was a hot and humid day, but her shorts weren't as short as most girls he had seen during his brief time in New Brick. But on a woman with her height, her attire left nothing to the imagination. Her black tank top was modest, but again it was worn by Aurora. Her tall, slender beauty would look good, better than good, on the cover of his magazine.

Out of the corner of his eye, he saw a man limping toward them, a furious expression on his face. The man grabbed her arm. "Rori, what the hell kinda stunt are you pulling embarrassing me?"

Guy saw her tense, and he acted before thinking. Pulling her away from the man's grasp, he gave the guy a threatening stare. "Who are you, and why do you think you can talk to my client this way?"

The man before him sputtered, his small eyes darting to Rori, "I'm Dwayne Tealy. Rori, who is this?"

Guy gave her a hopeful look. "I'm Guy Matthews, Rori's new editor."

She struggled at his words, but he leaned in and whispered in her ear, "Just go with it."

The man turned a shade of red. "Is this true?" he asked her. "Are you starting a new job?"

She shrugged. "Absolutely. And what business is it of yours anyway, Dwayne?"

Dwayne sputtered, "Well. How long has this been going on?'

Guy jumped in before she could speak. "We met two months ago at the shoot in Indiana and started discussing Rori's new career options then." He knew she had gone to this match, having watched part of her performance online, and hoped this disgruntled man hadn't attended the competition as well. Dwayne shifted from side to side and kept staring at them.

Evidently, he hadn't gone to the shoot.

Guy added, "Rori, we need to go so you can make your appointment." She looked up at him with disbelieving blue eyes, and he thought for a second she would admit they were lying.

"You're right, boss. We need to leave." She turned away

from him and dismissed the troublemaker with ease. "Again, good day, Dwayne."

They both watched as Dwayne stomped off in a temper toward his car.

"What's his problem?"

She shrugged her shoulders, "Same old, same old. Besides, I had it covered. You didn't need to step in like a knight on a white horse."

"Fine. You had it covered. Do you know if he's still watching us from his car?" He touched her arm with his fingers to stop her from turning. "No, don't turn around. Don't give him the satisfaction. You said you wanted to hear more about my offer?"

She started to shake her head, so he jumped in with more incentive. "Did I mention free items from *Stock and Guns* for life?" Oh man, out of all the things he had been saying, ammo talk seemed to stop her in her tracks.

He watched as she tossed her long, blond ponytail over her shoulder and stared up at him with those deep blue eyes. "Seriously? For as long as I live, anything out of your magazine, as much as I want?"

*Damn.* He hadn't thought this through, but the offer was already out there, and he wasn't about to take it back. "Of course, as much as you want."

The board would probably balk, but he had hit the magazine award lottery with Rori. If they could get her under contract before any of their competition caught wind of her, the cost of the inventory would be insignificant. The other magazine had been producing covers with famous top female shooters, and this was their chance to sponsor and promote their own up-and-coming female. She already had a small following on her blog, and with the right connections, she would do well in the future.

Waiting for her response took all the willpower he possessed. What was going on in her stubborn head?

"Ok. You make valid points. I'll hear you out. Meet me tomorrow night at the Pizza Grill. Six o'clock, and don't be late."

He reached into his khakis, pulled out his business card, and extended it to her. "In case you have any questions before tomorrow evening." Their fingers touched for a moment, and he felt a small jolt of something go through him.

She stuck the card in her pocket, and then used her long legs to jump into the cab of her truck. She roared the engine to life and took off without a backward glance. From the blaring of her stereo, he could make out an eighties rock-n-roll tune. *Mötley Crüe?* She was definitely his type of chick. Guy stood in the gravel parking lot staring after Rori's pickup as it kicked up dust on the dirt road. Waiting until tomorrow night might just kill him.

# CHAPTER TWO

Astonished she'd dealt with Dwayne, received a job offer, and met the most handsome man she'd ever laid eyes on all in the same day, Rori carelessly tossed her range bag on the floor of her gun room. Her condo was a small two bedroom, but instead of a guest room, she used the second bedroom as her office/gun room.

Still upset about the way Dwayne had ambushed her at the range, she plopped down beside her bag, but again rose to her feet as she remembered the cool shower and glass of wine she had been dying for earlier.

*Crap. Will this day never end?* Before comfort came the responsibility of cleaning and locking up her gear. The gun room was complete with charging docks for all her police force equipment and a large, top-of-the-line, Liberty gun safe—a graduation gift from her father. She usually enjoyed the process of cleaning and safely storing her weapons, but after this fiasco of an afternoon, she wanted to rush through the process as quickly as possible.

Thinking about this afternoon, her mind immediately went to Guy Matthews. Guy. What kind of first name was that anyway? And why did the bumping of their fingers and his smile leave her wanting more? Just thinking about his sexy smile, her stomach dropped again. There was a heat she hadn't felt in a long time. That man was too handsome for his own good.

Flattered and a bit nervous about his statement that he followed her shooting career, she both dreaded and looked forward to tomorrow evening. She intended to listen to his offer, but how could she accept? If circumstances were different...but they weren't. And they probably never would be.

The traveling all over the country bit sounded appealing, but not possible when she needed to be close to her dad here in New Brick. And, of course, she had a full-time job. A demanding one too. *Stick with the plan.* Yes, her original plan to stay by her dad for as long as he needed her was still her number one goal. Wondering about what could have been was a waste of time and energy.

And, she needed time and energy for the upcoming fall. She was still working toward saving enough money to take an online course in journalism. She'd eyed the class for so long, she hated to take on other responsibilities that could prevent her from achieving her goal. Even if she never used the degree, she had started something four years ago and didn't like the idea of starting something and never finishing.

Blowing her hair out of her face in frustration, she finished cleaning her Glock 17, locked it up, and shut the safe door. She turned around and admired her little gun room, appreciating the order, the detail. It calmed her, soothed her, to have things in order. Especially in her line of work.

At the door, Rori admired the light switch, shaped like a pistol—it added a quirky touch, she thought. She even had a gun lamp. Again, courtesy of her father.

One could never let the man know of any likes or collections. With his computer skills, he could ferret out the oddest gifts. He had called earlier today and said he had something great to show her.

Pondering what new, fascinating thing her dad had to show her tonight after dinner, Rori turned off the lights to her gun room and shut the door. Although she didn't need to check on him as she had right after her mom passed away, she did enjoy her father's company and was glad they still had each other. They were the only Crosses left. No aunts, uncles, or cousins.

The Cross family was one of the founding families of New Brick. All the men in the Cross family had served on the NBPD. Unfortunately, the Cross men usually didn't make it past the age of fifty. Heart disease was a terrible curse on the family, and due to that fact, Rori and her father were the only two remaining family members. It was also one of the reasons she came back home after her mom died. The obligation to her father to join the force had been overwhelming.

Her conscience hadn't bothered her too much when she went away to college. Her mom had insisted she follow her dream. And her dad, well, he had listened to her mom. For the first time in her life, Rori had been free. No workout schedule, no timer, and for two blessed years she was just an average college student. She had an academic scholarship and didn't have to play sports, and college had turned into the break she hadn't recognized she needed.

Lately, she had been feeling the same restlessness she had her last year of high school. She loved New Brick, but she wanted to travel, see the sights, write, sing, dance, and laugh…

In her line of work, there wasn't much time, or reason, for any of those things. That's why the opportunity with Guy's magazine was tempting. If only he knew how much she wanted this opportunity. He could have her squirming in her seat tomorrow night.

She imagined other things he could do to could make her squirm. Just thinking of those things made her skin grow warm…and his smile. *Damn that perfect smile.*

The sound of her cell phone beeping reminded her what time it was. *Wine would have to wait.* If she didn't get a move on, she was going to be late for dinner at her dad's.

Lateness was a weakness. And she had never been called weak.

* * *

"Ok, Mr. Editor, tell me about this big opportunity you mentioned yesterday."

She didn't waste any time, Guy thought to himself.

Again…his type of woman.

Also, the fact she was removing a Kevlar vest with one hand

16

while sipping a Redd's ale with the other. He had arrived right on time, and she hadn't taken the time to change from work.

Guy didn't know much about police work, but he suspected most officers removed the Kevlar before they walked into a bar and grill. Glancing around, Guy saw several men doing the same thing as Rori. The Pizza Grill appeared to be the after-hours hang out of the NBPD. They must all wear bullet-proof vests when out in the field. The short shooting bio he had read on her blog said she had joined the force four years ago, at the age of twenty. Although she had only been in law enforcement for four years, she had done the Glock circuit for over a year and had really been blowing away the competition. At her rate of growth, she would have the police force asking her which position she wanted, not the other way around.

Absorbed in his thoughts of her, Guy hadn't realized he was staring until she said abruptly, "At least your eyes are staring at my face."

Ouch. He wasn't sure what to say and tried to be diplomatic. "I'm sure it's hard being a woman in a man's line of work."

Her right eyebrow rose a fraction. "And what should I be doing, Mr. Matthews? Are you of the belief that women should be at home, in the kitchen, barefoot and pregnant?"

She didn't give him a chance to defend himself and fired another question right back at him. "Did you study law? You have the lawyer tone down." Another sip of beer passed her lips.

Alright, Guy, focus on her eyes, not her lips. "No, I didn't study law. How about you?"

"Oh, no, Mr. Editor, I want to interrogate you. See, I ask,

and you answer. Understand?" He wasn't used to a woman speaking without a lot of hand gestures or head movements.

He did understand. This woman was gaining the upper hand. She wanted to take control, which was fine by him, and he let her. He leaned back on his barstool and extended his arms. "Sweetheart. I'm all yours. Ask away."

Did he just imagine her quick inhalation? Maybe the woman before him wasn't as hard as nails after all.

"Umm, ok, I know *Stock and Guns* is located in Wyoming, but where?"

Ahh, she was easy on him and taking the impersonal approach. "Well, the magazine is published in Cheyenne, but we have a warehouse in Jackson, as well, where the orders are filled and shipped. There is a connected studio where the art department puts together the spreads and the writers send in their contributions. Question number two, please."

Her face showed it all. Interest. More than interest.

He jumped right in and didn't give her time to ask question number two. He leaned on the table, his long arms almost touching hers. "You know, Rori. I think you would make an excellent addition to our SG team. With SG sponsoring you, the sky is the limit, for both parties."

She took another sip of her beer, probably stalling, "You think so, Mr. Matthews? The way I see it, you haven't offered me anything yet. Haven't told me what is required."

All of a sudden, she was serious. The earlier teasing "Mr. Editor-in-Chief" was replaced with professionalism. Time for him to get serious as well. He was not a salesman.

He proceeded to tell her about the offer. It would require

some travel and media spots, but he thought she would enjoy it. "Imagine the hit you'll be. You and only a handful of ladies in the country can do what you do. This could open doors for you that would take years to open otherwise. You could compete in matches all over the country, not just in your area."

She stared back at him intently. Was she waiting for more incentive? Then he stated, "You get to spend more time with me, and I'm sure I'll come in handy when you need someone to rescue you on a white horse."

She laughed, thinking he joked, but he didn't say anything, and she stopped abruptly. So, he pulled the contract out of his bag and pushed it across the high-top table. "Alright. Here is our offer, read through it, mark it up, and tell me what you like and don't like."

"I will. I'll call you when I'm done. I should go…"

"Stay and have dinner with me." She seemed to be mulling it over, and he could see her shift slightly on her barstool.

"Okay."

Surprised she agreed, he questioned, "Okay?" At her nod, he then asked, "Great, what do you like on your pizza?"

She laughed at him as if he was crazy. "Everything, of course."

He liked everything too and had to remind himself again this was a business dinner and not a first date.

Rori stared at him strangely and rose from her seat. "I'll just be a minute," she said and headed off toward the back of the restaurant.

Guy signaled the young waiter and put in their pizza order and two more beers. The beers arrived just as she returned. Was there a hint of lip-gloss on her lips? She didn't have on makeup yesterday when he met her and hadn't earlier today either.

She didn't need it.

Aurora Cross was a natural beauty. She sat down and took a drink, then opened the conversation back up with, "See this scar on my thumb? I got that scar the first time I went hunting with my dad."

He leaned in and held her hand to examine it more closely until an unwelcome visitor stopped at their table. Dwayne from yesterday at the shoot, but today he was wearing a police uniform.

The man sneered at them and said, "More PDA?"

Before Guy could stop her, Rori took her almost full beer and poured it over the man's head. She jumped down from her stool angrily. "Leave me alone, Dwayne."

Dwayne sputtered under the foam of light beer and was about to go after her when Guy stopped him by shoving him against the table. "Ok, little man. You're done here."

Dwayne opened his mouth to protest, but Guy gave him the look. The look that said, "Walk away or I hurt you." Guy held his breath for a second; he knew a police officer stood before him and how much trouble would follow if he laid one finger on Dwayne.

Luckily, his look worked. Dwayne wiped away the foam from his eyes and had to get the last word in. "This isn't over," he said. Guy had to stop himself from hitting the creep. Something was off with the dude.

He shot a quick glance at Rori. "You okay?"

"Just pissed off."

"You need to file a complaint about the prick."

She laughed. "I have, and I almost lost my job. I'm thankful I only got suspended over it."

"Want to talk about it?"

"He assaulted me at work after my dad pulled some strings to switch and have Henry as my partner instead of him. Henry and I grew up together, and we worked well together in the past…and Dwayne was just acting creepy."

"Assaulted?"

"Yes, it didn't get too far, since I 'assaulted' him right back. I kicked the crap out of him and broke his collarbone."

Guy was steaming, but he tried not to show it. "This is terrible, Rori."

She shrugged. "But nothing can be done. His father owns the entire town. He donates tons of money to everything and is the biggest employer in two counties. Plus, his mother is the mayor."

He thought about the new info for a second. "Ouch. Is Dwayne's father like him?"

She lifted her ponytail off her shoulder. "Actually, Dwayne's father is a nice man. Unfortunately, his mother is not. It is because of her Dwayne gets everything he wants."

He immediately thought of one of his favorite television shows. "Kind of like the Olesons."

He was getting ready to explain when she chimed in. "Yes, Dwayne is Nellie Oleson! I never thought of it that way before."

Surprised someone her age had watched *Little House on the Prairie*, he smiled widely. He could really fall for this woman. "So, tell me about your favorite episode."

She clearly knew the television show as well as he did and described a favorite scene that had struck a chord with her. He listened for a good ten minutes until their pizza arrived. He was about to dig in when she asked the waiter for a box.

"I have a better idea," she said. "Let's go back to my place, eat pizza, I'll pop some popcorn, and we can watch a movie."

He liked her way of thinking. "An action film?"

She laughed loudly. "Sure."

After a few minutes, the waiter showed up to box their pizza. Guy paid the bill amid her protests. While he balanced the pizza box on one hand, he helped her down from the stool. At first, she didn't know what he was doing, almost as if she had never had a man be a gentleman around her.

"I'll follow you," he said, holding open the exit door.

He pulled his rental car into the space next to her truck. She was full of surprises. Her home, a condo in a nice complex, was complete with pool, tennis courts, and other upscale amenities, he was sure. Why would a country girl like her be living in place like this? He imagined her with a large range in her backyard.

She opened her door and yelled rather than asked, "Are you coming?"

He chuckled at her lack of finesse. She just didn't give a damn. He liked it more and more. She was truly the best shooting talent he had ever found—no, that the magazine had ever found. No longer worried about the National Magazine Award, he would be glad just signing her because it was best for all parties.

In no time at all, she had beer, paper plates, napkins, and

popcorn on her rectangular wooden coffee table. She didn't mess around. "It's a good thing you were there tonight to save Dwayne. I was ready to kick his butt!"

She put the selected the movie in while turning on the surround sound. He imagined she could kick Dwayne's ass, but considered her approach.

"So, let me ask this…if I hadn't been there, how would you have done it?"

She moved so fast, he didn't even see what karate/ninja move she used. His legs were out from under him, and he landed with a thud on the floor. Only problem was he had grabbed something to hold onto and that something turned out to be her. Rori in all her glory. On top of him.

She was breathing fast, and her heart was beating rapidly. No, wait, *his* heart was beating rapidly. He stared up at those big blue eyes of hers and didn't do what he wanted to do, which was kiss her like crazy. Instead, he laughed.

Soon, she was laughing too. Sucking in much needed air, he said, "It's a good thing you didn't pull this move on Dwayne. It would have burst my ego."

Rori, laughing and slaphappy, pulled away from him a bit. "He still didn't get what he deserved, but that's another conversation. Now it's time for movie and pizza."

Rising, she held out her hand to Guy and pulled him to his feet. The motion seemed natural to her. He watched her walk to the couch. She sat down and propped her feet up and said, "Come on, Mr. Editor. Relax."

## CHAPTER THREE

"What do you mean Dwayne is missing?"

Rori had expected the mailman when she had hastily thrown on her old blue robe over her pajamas. Instead, she had opened her front door to two uniformed co-workers, Bill and Henry.

"Morning. What can I do for you fellas?"

Bill, Dwayne's partner, spoke first. "Dwayne hasn't shown up for work this morning. Our shift started at six o'clock. We tried his house and his parents' house. No Dwayne. You wouldn't happen to know anything about his whereabouts now, do ya?"

"Bill, a missing person can't be reported until it's been over twenty-four hours. It hasn't been twenty-four hours yet."

"Seeing as how you publicly humiliated him two days ago at the range and last night at the Pizza Grill, I reported it. Madam Mayor wanted him listed as missing since it is uncharacteristic

24

of her son to not show up for work or tell family where he is going. You are the number one suspect in his disappearance, and with your history, you have motive."

Bill adjusted himself then. Almost as big of a jerk as Dwayne, she ignored his rudeness and turned her attention to Henry, her current partner, and the only friend left from high school she still spoke to.

"Henry, I know this doesn't look good, but I'm not the only one with motive. Half the force would give their right hand to have Dwayne gone. You know me…"

Henry fidgeted with his notepad and pen. "Don't come in today, Rori, and don't leave the county."

"Bullshit," she said bluntly before reining in her anger. She tightened the belt on her robe and sighed. "Sorry for the bad news, but you know I had nothing to do with this." Both shifted uneasily from side to side.

Bill had one last question before he was ready to leave. "We've already checked with Dwayne's cell phone provider, and the last signal from his phone occurred at one o'clock this morning. You got an alibi for one a.m.?"

She did have an alibi, but she wasn't about to offer it, so she just stared at both of them. The gossip surrounding her over the last month had been enough. She wasn't saying anything else to start the rumor mill back up. Henry and Bill dropped eye contact and looked at their feet instead. A lot of "uh's" were uttered, but not much else. Eventually, she won the stare-down contest, and her two co-workers turned around and headed back to their squad car.

A sleepy-sounding voice called out to her. "Rori?"

She turned and found Guy sprawled on her couch. They had been dead to the world last night. Both had fallen asleep during the second movie, but she had stirred around midnight. She hadn't been in the mood to wake him after their little wrestling match.

Those dark eyes of his upon her in the wee hours of the morning while she was vulnerable? Oh, hell no! She had opted out of wakening those emotions. Not sure she wouldn't have begged him to take her just as all those wanton heroines did in the romance novels she loved to read.

So, she had left him sleeping. Plus, she figured a night on her couch wouldn't hurt anybody. Never had she imagined the whole town would find out about this. New Brick fit the stereotype as far as small-town gossip went. It was just like any other small town. Single women, police officers especially, toed the line.

How the heck could she explain this? Her dad would *not* be pleased when he found out her alibi was a stranger she had just met two days ago. This stranger was now burning a hole in her back. She could feel him staring at her. Frustrated, she called over her shoulder to him. "Yeah, Guy."

"That's the first time you called me by my first name. Are you sick?"

It was a teasing question, but she felt its undercurrent. "No, but I am staying home from work today."

He looked at her expectantly, and she told him about Dwayne's disappearance. "Well, did you tell them you had an alibi?"

She gave him a dumb look and shrugged her shoulders but

said nothing.

"You didn't tell them because you didn't want them to know I was here. I'm right, aren't I?"

"My dad is old-fashioned, and he wouldn't think last night was innocent. He would probably demand a shotgun wedding."

Guy laughed at her.

"You don't know my dad. Edward Cross is the most determined, single-minded person on this planet. And he expects me, his only child, to approach life the same way."

As a little girl, she hadn't wanted pink tutus and ballet lessons. Instead, she had wanted to be with her father. Target practice, hunting, fishing—he had even coached her tennis and archery teams.

She had become the son he'd always wanted. She had wanted to prove to herself she could do anything boys could do. So, she had pushed herself and sometimes let her father push her even harder in every sport she attempted. Improving her speed and coordination while her father timed her, he pressured her until her mom would step in and kindly tell him to back off a bit.

It was only when her mom had insisted on some "girl time" with her daughter that Edward would stop practice, since he denied his dear wife nothing. Those girly times with her mom involved lots of pedicures, movies, and laughter.

Rori had told her dad she wasn't into the girly stuff with her mom, and she did it to make Sallie happy. Secretly, though, she had treasured those moments. She had been free to feel like a young girl, watch romances, and paint her toes. She had appreciated her father wanted to help her so much, but sometimes she had just wanted to put on a dress and have her dad take her to the father-daughter dinners their church hosted. She had never asked to go, and her father had never offered to take her.

So, she had learned to be the perfect tomboy. She did all the sports and competitions her dad wanted and all the frilly, fun things her mom wanted. Oh, how she missed her mom.

"Rori? Are you okay?"

*Guy.* She had forgotten he was there, lost in the past. She wasn't about to tell Guy about her mom. Raw with emotion, she pushed aside memories of her mom and instead said, "Just thinking about my dad's reaction to this news. He is going to have a fit. You think I'm joking, Mr. Matthews. I'm not. I have dinner with my dad tonight. I must tell him before one of my neighbors does. I'm not sure what to tell him."

"Tell him the truth. Would it help if I went along to smooth things over? I'm great at interrogation."

He looked so sincere, even with the tumbled dark hair and crumpled clothing.

Delicious.

She just bet he was great at smoothing things over. She immediately thought of his hand smoothing her hair out of her face last night. Putting on her best interrogation face, she looked at him. "You'll do anything to get me to sign the contract won't you?"

He would do anything to get her to sign the contract.

Even stand next to her dad while he held a loaded gun after

they had told Mr. Cross about him spending the night on Rori's couch. Needless to say, she had been right about her father's reaction. While there may not be a shotgun wedding, a mad father holding a gun couldn't go well for him.

"Sir, sure is a nice Glock M course you have there." He should have been speechless, or scared, but he was neither. Instead, he was complimenting her father on his target practices set up down a path in their woods.

The Cross homestead was a few miles from town. The property was an old farm with lots of unused pasture and old outbuildings. The large white house had an abundance of windows and porches. He could make out multiple unkempt flower beds, and he speculated as to what had happened to make the place so dismal. Lack of finances? Lack of time?

Edward Cross had served them dinner, then taken him out to see his guns and his courses. Rori had stayed behind to clean up and promised to join them soon. Guy believed she was nervous and cleaning up was her way out of this tense situation.

Edward, a tall, lean man, went on to describe the courses in detail. "The Glock M is measured exactly as it is in competition. And so is the Five to Glock course on down the path. It is important for Aurora to have a private place to practice for her competitions."

Edward was not what Guy had been expecting. He was serious and factual. He addressed his daughter by her full first name, never her nickname. Which Guy found odd. He also learned Rori practiced most nights after dinner with her father. In fact, she had been practicing with her father since she was thirteen. Why did she only start competing a year ago?

Apparently, most of her life had involved some type of competition. Her father had coached her in every sport she had ever played. She had excelled at all of them. Guy had the impression Edward Cross believed his daughter's ability was his own achievement. The way he trained his daughter, not any God-given talent or personal determination on her part.

"How's it going?"

He turned to see Rori standing there with a questioning look on her face. She seemed to be holding back, waiting for the next shoe to drop—the first one had dropped during dinner when her father had questioned the two them over the previous night.

"Your father was just showing me his courses. You seem to have the perfect place to practice." He thought he should keep it cool so she wouldn't know Edward was trying to freak him out.

"Aurora, show him how this course should be done. After, let's see if he can do any better." Edward had put him in for punishment—intimidation hadn't worked, but a stomping given by his daughter may just do it.

"Dad, is this really necessary? Guy has seen this type of course before..." she started, but her father cut her off with a glare. He wasn't sure why, but Guy had the overwhelming urge to snap at Edward Cross. His protectiveness of this young woman just kept growing. Not only did he defend her in front of an entire restaurant, he had played possum on her couch so he could stay and keep an eye on her. He had known she wouldn't dare wake him, and he didn't trust her sneaky co-worker as far as he could throw him.

Rori flipped her ponytail and sauntered toward them. "Fine, Dad." She stepped up to the assembly table and put on hearing and eye protection. Quickly, she loaded her magazine, aimed at each target, and did a dry-run before her father started the timer. After Edward hit the button, she was quick and dead-on. Even in her own backyard during a friendly competition, she gave it her all. She had to be the best shooter he had ever seen.

"Mr. Matthews, you're up." Edward grinned from ear to ear.

Guy's stomach dropped. It had been a while since he had practiced. While he knew he could never come close to Rori, he didn't want to look like a complete imbecile either.

Stepping up to the table, he used the earplugs and glasses Edward handed him. After putting on both, he shoved the loaded magazine into the 17 provided. He aimed at the targets, waited for Edward's signal, gave a nod of his head, and let it rip.

Shooting was like riding a bike. He didn't do it often as he was busy with his business, but his body never forgot. The surge of adrenaline coursing through his veins, the kickback that he always expected, the feeling of accomplishment as those targets went down.

Every time reminded him of the first time in his friend Brock's backyard and how a whole new world had opened for him. Brock would enjoy seeing Rori shoot. On second thought, he didn't want single, womanizing Brock to meet her. Ever. Brock would steal her away from him. Wait. Guy could hold his own with the ladies. He was sure Rori wouldn't fall for Brock's one-liners, although his best friend could write a book full of them.

"Boy, are you done staring at those targets?"

Guy snapped back to reality. He had been standing looking at the fallen targets for who knew how long. "Sorry, sir, it's been a while since I've practiced. I was just admiring the fact that I still remember how to shoot."

"Well, don't admire too much. I know nine-year-olds with more skill than you."

A chuckle drew his attention to Rori. She quickly covered her mouth with her hand, but Guy could see her eyes shining. She was striking, and he wanted nothing more than to see what she had on underneath her denim shorts and white tank top. Her style was simple, but she certainly didn't need to wear anything fancy to draw men to her.

He remembered this morning, Rori standing before him in an old robe, long, tan legs bare and bunny slippers on her feet. It should have turned him off, but it hadn't. Her long, blond hair had been down, and the robe had almost been sheer. If she only knew what he was thinking at this moment, she would probably turn and run back into her father's house.

Edward snapped his fingers in front of Guy's face. "Stop gawking at my daughter and get on with your shooting."

After spending the night on his daughter's couch and getting caught undressing her with his eyes, he would have kissed Edward's feet to get on the man's good side. "Yes, sir."

"And stop calling me sir. It makes me feel like an old man. Call me Edward."

Guy and Rori finished the courses as Edward timed them. As expected, she beat him by several seconds each time, and even longer on the plates when his gun jammed. Nothing like getting beat by a girl. But that didn't bother him. His masculinity was not on trial here, and he grasped the very thing that most men were jealous of about her, he found attractive.

The three of them loaded up the range bags and gathered the shells and headed back to the house. Rori pulled a pie out of the fridge, and she'd already had coffee brewed. She was in the process of serving them when Guy jumped up to help her.

"Here, you cleaned up dinner. Let me do this." Their hands brushed as he took the coffee pot from her. He placed a hand on her shoulder and guided her into the padded kitchen chair.

She opened her mouth wide and seemed genuinely stunned. Apparently, she was used to her role of son, daughter, and maid to her father. He recalled that last night she had everything in place for their pizza and movie night before he could blink an eye.

He watched her as she grabbed the contract he had given her the night before and pushed it toward her father. "Dad, I want you to read the offer Guy has made me. Of course, most of the travel is out of the question, but I feel it is something to consider."

Taking a sip of the coffee Guy placed before him, Edward flipped through the contract. A stall tactic he recognized since he used the same one during negotiations. Edward then pulled his reading glasses from his breast pocket and started reading.

Guy looked toward Rori and noticed she was chewing her lip. Her father's approval meant a great deal to her. He felt he should offer more incentive. "Edward, I would also like to take you and Rori out to Wyoming and show you both the warehouse. Give you the grand tour and let you see what *Stock and Guns* is all about before you all decide. Also, I'm sure your lawyer will need time to look this over, as well."

The offer seemed to have Edward thinking hard, but then he

said, "Aurora can't go anywhere until this mess with Dwayne is cleared up."

He saw her close her eyes briefly. This was something she really wanted. But he could wait—he was the boss.

"I'll be in town for a while then. I would like to personally escort both of you out West. Have either of you ever been?" After a negative answer from both, he went on to describe his ranch and the magazine business. Both seemed interested, and he noticed Edward was writing down a few things in the notepad he had pulled out of his shirt pocket. The man's pocket was a bottomless pit.

The three of them fell into an easy conversation, enjoying coffee and pie. Guy learned more and more about Rori. It seemed he had it all wrong earlier. She had wanted to excel, and her father just supplied her with the best instruction he could provide.

It was good to hear her laugh, and to hear Edward tell about how brave she had been during their first hunting trip when she had cut her hand. She had needed stitches, but she hadn't cried once.

Did she ever cry?

His mother was a psychologist, and she had taught him it was healthy to have a good cry now and then. His father, the heart surgeon, agreed. Even though Guy's childhood wasn't all roses, he couldn't imagine never being able to cry, being praised for not letting your true emotions show.

As he looked across the small kitchen table and into Rori's deep blue eyes, he realized he wanted his shoulder to be the one she cried on.

## CHAPTER FOUR

T he sun was hot, like the book Rori was reading. Day two of her restriction from work was turning out to be a pleasant little vacation day for her. She lounged on a chaise by her community pool, soaking up the rays and catching up with her reading.

The current romance novel involved a tall, dark, and handsome highwayman. She envisioned the highwayman looked like Guy and the heroine in the novel resembled her.

She couldn't even read a simple book without getting all hot and bothered thinking about him. Disgusted, she slid her bookmark in place and headed for the diving board.

She executed a perfect dive, and when she surfaced, was met with applause. Wiping the water from her face, she tilted her head up and saw Guy smiling down at her. His smile undid her. It made her want to do things—things that nice, well-bred ladies didn't do. It was a good thing she had never considered herself a lady, much to her neighbors' chagrin.

What would he do if she got out of this pool, grabbed him, and smothered his handsome face with kisses as she ran her hands all over his...

"Hi," he called out. "Are you good at everything you do?"

Darn. The man of her dreams interrupted her naughty daydream. His smile was contagious. She couldn't help but laugh at his question. "Of course not. I can't cook and I'm terrible with computers." She swam to the ladder and climbed out of the pool.

He held a towel out, wrapping it securely around her, then turned her, still holding on to the edges near her throat. Inhaling deeply, she could smell his aftershave. The man even smelled delicious.

"I can cook. How about I make us some lunch?"

Darn it. She had been expecting a kiss, or a hug, but not an offer for lunch. This was business for him. She mustn't forget that.

"Umm, sure." *Focus*.

First, she stepped away from Guy, so she could think. He distracted her. He dropped his hands from the towel, but then he brushed her wet hair away from her face. The man was killing her.

"You go shower and get dressed, and I'll run to the grocery and come back here and make the best lunch you have ever eaten."

She scoffed. "I'm sure you are exaggerating. My mom was an excellent cook." He tilted his head and looked at her strangely. She knew he was going to start asking questions and she wasn't ready to answer them.

"That is the first time you have ever mentioned your mom."

Not the comment she had been expecting. She could defuse this conversation before it became uncomfortable for her. "Yeah, it hurts to talk about her. Listen, you go shopping, and I'll head back to the condo." She gathered up her book and shoved it in the small tote she used for the pool. "See you in a bit."

\* \* \*

Guy watched her gather her things and noticed something new about her appearance. Rori's feet were slim just like the rest of her, but the bit of glitter caught his eye. Jewels on each of her big toes were set atop hot pink polish. He was surprised because she didn't wear any jewelry and her fingernails were always neatly trimmed and bare of any polish.

She gave him a little wave and hustled toward her condo. He walked to his rental car in the parking lot, thinking hard about his exchange with her. What happened to her mom? Neither Edward nor Rori had mentioned her passing or even her name.

When he had first met her, he thought she was a tough opponent. Knowing she had a weak spot didn't make her any less tough in his eyes. He was glad she had shown him her softer side.

If he could understand this emotional side of her, maybe he could understand why her eyes lit up when he talked about Wyoming and the contract. She wanted this badly, but he thought something else was making her hesitate besides this tangle with Dwayne.

For now, he had lunch to prepare.

Thirty minutes later, he arrived back at her condo with his arms full. She must have been waiting because the door opened before he could ring the bell. She had changed into black shorts, a pink tank top, and flip-flops. Her face was bare of makeup, and her hair was pulled back into her usual ponytail.

"What are we having?"

"I plan on surprising you. Go sit while I cook."

He had picked up fresh vegetables and the fixings for jambalaya. Since she didn't cook, he didn't know what kind of kitchen set-up she had. So, something simple but tasty would do.

Rori had pulled bottles of water out of the fridge and was in the process of pouring them into glasses full of ice. "You seem comfortable in the kitchen."

"I had to be with my doctor parents' work schedules, and then at college living with my friend Brock. He thinks opening a can is cooking."

"Well, isn't it?"

"No, and you and Brock can never meet."

She threw her head back and laughed. "Why is that?"

"You two have too much in common. Brock doesn't cook, he doesn't take shit from anyone, and his shooting skills are up there with the best. I don't know, but the two of you may be too busy trying to outdo each other. Maybe I shouldn't be worried."

He told her about his history with the Walker family. "I met Brock Walker almost twenty years ago on my first day of high school. It had been the first time I had attended public school. Brock had walked right up to me, shook my hand, introduced himself, and that was that.

"I got into guns because of Brock and his family. I had never even been close to a gun, let alone shot one. That first day, out in Brock's backyard target practicing, introduced me to a brand-new world. It involved the entire family, even his little sister."

"Would you really be worried about my meeting Brock?" Out of all the information he had just revealed to her, this tidbit must have stuck with her. Not ready to let her in on his feelings just yet, he said, "Yes, I'd be worried. He would try to romance you, and I can't have that while we are working on a business deal." Stirring the jambalaya, he watched her exhale deeply as if she had been holding her breath. *Damn it.*

She recovered quickly and said, "I wouldn't worry if I were you. I think I can resist Brock."

He hoped so, as he planned on taking her to Wyoming as soon as possible. "We will see." Brock, a notorious womanizer with three failed engagements, didn't need to put the moves on her. Guy couldn't let that happen. If for one second Brock thought Rori was a free agent, his friend would be all over her. He couldn't have that and would have to think of a way to stop Brock from advancing full force.

"Do you need help with the salad? I can chop at least." Rori interrupted his thoughts of Brock and seduction plans. Guy wouldn't let them meet until he had the situation under control.

"Sure. I didn't know what you liked in your salad, so I just picked up a bit of everything." She stepped behind him, and he thought for a second that she had stopped to inhale his cologne. No, he was just being hopeful.

She stood next to him and chopped like an expert. "Hey, I thought you didn't know how to cook."

"I can't, but I didn't say I didn't know how to chop. That was my job in the kitchen growing up. I chopped, and dad cleaned up."

He noticed how she didn't mention her mom and let it ride. "That sounds like a good team effort. My meals were usually prepared by our housekeeper and then frozen. So, after I learned how to cook, that task was delegated to me."

Still chopping away, she said, "So you didn't mind the responsibility?"

"No, not at all. Gave me some responsibility for the first time in my life. We lived in town, so I didn't have the chore of mowing the lawn. The housekeeper took care of everything inside. So, cooking for our family actually got me away from the television."

"You weren't involved in any sports?"

"Nope. I was a husky kid in school."

The knife she was using slipped and almost cut her finger. "I'm sorry. You are so fit now, it is hard to imagine you as ever being unhealthy." She picked up the cutting board and slid the chopped veggies into the big bowl she had pulled out of the cabinet.

He could get used to this—working side by side in her kitchen seemed normal. As if they prepared meals in her kitchen daily. "Yes, I was an overweight kid until the summer before high school. I shot up several inches, and we moved to

Wyoming. I met Brock that first day of school and I have been trying to keep up with him ever since."

Rori carried the salad bowl to her small, two-seater table. "So, in a way Brock was your personal trainer?" She returned to his side, pulled down plates from the upper cabinet above her head, and then scooped up the cutlery out the drawer. Since her condo was in a newer community, her kitchen had all the bells and whistles—granite countertops, top-of-the-line cabinets, and stainless-steel appliances.

"I guess you could say that, but he did more than keep me away from the television and the fridge, he introduced me to the great outdoors. This continued through college. When I started working for *Stock and Guns,* Brock provided some of the best ideas for my articles."

That seemed to awaken something in her. "I love your articles."

"You do?" She sat motionless and just stared at him. "What is it? What's wrong?"

"I went to the University of Maryland, but I wasn't able to finish." She studied her hands. Guy had learned a few things about her in the short time he'd known her, and she wasn't a quitter. Something or someone had forced her away from college.

"Do you ever think about going back to college? Or changing careers? This seems like something you really wanted to do."

She shrugged, but when she looked up at him with those big blue eyes, he felt his heart tearing just a bit. "Maybe in future. But as far as changing careers, that is impossible. The Cross family has a long history of being on the New Brick Police Force. *And* I'm good at what I do."

"Rori, I think you could be great at whatever you set your mind to, but is your heart in it? Do you enjoy waking up to another day of police work?"

"It doesn't matter what my heart wants, Guy. This is what I do, all I'll ever do. Listen, I don't want to sound like some lame daddy's girl complaining about her life. Let's talk about something else."

She moved by him to collect the plates to set out on the table. He reached out and placed his hands on her shoulders. "Wait. I know I have only known you a few days, but for some reason it seems like I have known you a lifetime. I'm sorry if I misspoke and made you uncomfortable."

He waited for her response, but it seemed like an eternity. He gently massaged her shoulders as she finally replied.

"I feel the same way, that I have known you much longer than a few days. I don't know how to explain it, but I trust you." That simple statement tore the rest of his heart wide open. He had guessed that trust didn't come easily to her and, as always, she surprised him with her strength.

"Well, if you trust me, how about you sit down and eat the best jambalaya that has ever passed your lips." He rubbed her bottom lip before quickly stepping away and getting their lunch on the table.

Conversation during lunch turned to hunting tales. She told stories that some little girls would never experience—sitting in a camouflage pop-up blind all day, holding her bladder for hours, bow and arrow at the ready, as she waited for her first ten-point buck. After five hours, she had gotten the buck, not a ten-point, but she had only been seven years old.

The hunting tales stopped when her cell phone began to vibrate on the counter. She rose and answered it.

"Hello. Yeah, Dad. Hmm, I'm at home having lunch with Guy."

She paused as she waited on her dad to speak. "Do you really need me there? Sure. Yes, I hadn't thought about that. I'll be there in thirty minutes."

She had a frown on her face when she disconnected the call. He was tempted to kiss her just then. She was adorable, even when she frowned.

"Anything wrong?"

"No, just the Main Street Festival, it takes place every July. Dad feels that I should come down and help him at his historical society booth and prove my innocence instead of hiding out at home."

He stood and began to stack the dishes on top of each other. "Then I will come down and help too."

"Seriously, you don't have to waste your time with our little festival. Dad just wants me to be visible. He doesn't need the extra hands." She took the dishes from him and began rinsing them off and loading them in the dishwasher.

He covered the leftover lunch and placed it in the fridge. "Rori, in case you haven't noticed, I enjoy your company. Plus, if there is any trouble, you may need a big, strong man around."

"In that case, I need to call someone else."

Shocked for a moment, he quickly realized that she was

teasing him. "Just for that, I refuse to make the chocolate dessert I'd planned."

She mocked him again and did her best impression of being shot through the heart. "Oh, you know where to hit a girl, don't you? Okay, then. Guy, please come with me and stomp on spiders and do whatever else big, strong men do."

\* \* \*

This year was the first time she had ever had a man accompany her to the festival. She had to admit, it felt nice having Guy by her side. The Main Street Festival was one of her favorite summertime events in New Brick. The flags hanging from the lamp posts, the brightly colored flowers up and down the side-walks. She loved New Brick, she really did. She just didn't want to spend her entire life here.

Rori had thought this a million times, but never vocalized it. She came close to telling Guy, though. Telling him all her wants, dreams, desires…things that she knew she couldn't have. Not now.

She pointed out old buildings as they walked along. Once they left her truck, he held her hand and asked questions about the town.

She could get used to this…walking side-by-side with this handsome man.

Her first impression of him had been wrong. She could admit that now. He did something to her when he was around. She trusted him unlike anyone else. It was surprising and shocking even, considering their short acquaintance.

"There's Edward." Guy pulled her over toward her father's booth.

Her dad looked like the absent-minded professor. He was sweating, and he had a bit of dirt on his cheek, which she wiped away.

"So, you brought some extra hands. Great. Guy, I have several boxes to unload and these old arms are tired of packing. Would you be so kind to get them for me?"

Her dad shouldn't carry heavy items, but that had never stopped him before, so that meant he wanted Guy out of the way for a moment. After Guy was beyond hearing distance, she asked, "Dad, what is it?"

Edward looked from side to side, "Dwayne's mother is on the prowl and she is being noisy. I needed you here to combat those rumors. Aurora, you've been sulking, which is not like you at all. What is going on?"

Crap, leave it to her father to know she was sulking. "Nothing, Dad. Can't I just have a day off to enjoy myself? Don't worry about Jeanette Tealy, I will handle it."

"Aurora, that's what I'm worried about. Your behavior since Dwayne has been missing is uncharacteristic. You need to be out there proving your innocence. You must be careful in this situation. I may not be able to help you out of this pickle, so you need to be visible, and keep your eyes open."

"Thanks for the warning, Dad." She didn't need a warning about Jeanette Tealy. She was the biggest pain in the ass, besides Dwayne, she'd ever met.

Rumor had it, Jeanette had a hard childhood and her husband, Charles, overlooked many of her actions because of it.

He even bought her position as mayor. Rori just thought it was an excuse so he wouldn't have to divide his fortune in half if he divorced Jeanette.

Guy returned with his arms full of boxes and proceeded to unpack them on the table her father had indicated. The boxes contained brochures, old framed photographs, postcards, and other items for display and purchase. Guy was really getting to her. Every action showed her what a nice man he truly was.

"Edward, how about a cold beverage? Rori, anything for you?" He looked down at her, and she couldn't speak for a moment. Edward, of course, needed—not wanted—a sweet iced tea. Her father thought mid-Ohio was the Deep South.

"Thanks, but no thanks." As she watched him walk toward the vending booths, she appreciated his backside. Oh yes, she appreciated his long, lean, slightly hairy legs, firm butt, and large, broad shoulders. She could spend a long while with her limbs wrapped up with his.

It had been a long time since her one and only boyfriend at college. In her mind he was "the bastard." He didn't have a name, as she refused to utter it or think it. One miserable experience at college had increased her belief men were not to be trusted. And yet, here she was, trusting an almost complete stranger. Telling him about her college dreams, almost telling him about the painful loss of her mom.

Where was her loyalty to her dad and the police force? If it weren't for the mess with Dwayne right now, would she be on a plane to Wyoming?

She doubted she could give up a trip to see how one of her favorite magazines came to fruition every month. This could be a life-altering event. The chance to switch to a career she loved, instead of one she merely liked. Yeah, she would do it. She should tell Guy that as soon as she was cleared to leave the county she wanted to go with him to Wyoming. In fact, she was going to find him and tell him now.

Turning to her father, she said, "I'm going to go help Guy carry back the drinks."

He gave her a knowing smile. "I figured you would with the way you were staring a hole into his back."

She did have the grace to blush but quickly hurried in Guy's direction. She thought she saw him at a distance but then lost him. She cut behind some of the vending trailers and right in front of her was Dwayne Tealy. *What the hell?*

Her instincts didn't remember she was wearing flip-flops, and she took off after him. She chased him yelling, "*Stop!*" trying to draw attention to them.

As she ran after him, she thought that running might be the only thing the weasel could best her in. She was fast, but he was smaller and quicker. He maneuvered around barrels and cars and headed off of Main Street to the old industrial park. She chased him toward several buildings that were currently under renovation. These buildings belonged to Dwayne's father, and he knew them like the back of his hand.

Sure enough, he ran into the first building on his left, and she entered right behind him. He darted around columns and debris left by construction workers. She caught up to him and grabbed the back of his t-shirt, but he spun around and grabbed her ponytail, elbowing her in the face.

They went down on the concrete floor. Dwayne straddled

her and held his arm to her throat. Dazed from the elbow to her face, she felt him hover over her as he muttered, "We could've owned this town."

She might be down, but she wasn't about to let him win. She said, "You're crazy," and poked him in the left eye.

He retaliated by adding pressure on her throat.

She focused on trying to breathe and heard footsteps running toward them.

"Stop!" At the sound of a male voice, Dwayne stopped.

He levered off her as she struggled to sit up and turn to see who approached them. Dwayne pulled out his gun, aimed, shot, and ran.

The footsteps belonged to Guy. Still sitting on the concrete floor, Rori watched Guy whiz by her.

Dwayne hadn't hit him. Guy slowed, then turned back and crouched down beside her, anger and concern showing on his face as he took in the bruise starting on her cheek. He helped her to her feet and put his arms around her. She felt safe within his embrace.

She leaned her aching face into his shoulder. "He shot at you," she croaked.

He shrugged dismissively. "He missed."

Guy leaned down and tilted her cheek up for inspection, running his thumbs over the redness on her throat. She didn't want him to think she had gone soft on him. "I wasn't worried. Dwayne has terrible aim."

# CHAPTER FIVE

G uy was finally in his own bed and too wired to sleep.
The flight to Wyoming had felt like a lifetime instead of four short hours. Rori had laid her head on his shoulder and slept most of the trip.

He spent the four-hour flight trying to ignore her coconut-scented shampoo instead of working on his laptop. She didn't stir throughout the entire flight. Apparently, she always slept like the dead, which was strange considering her line of work. Based on a documentary he had once watched, police officers had to be ready at a moment's notice. Maybe she just felt comfortable and secure sleeping on his shoulder?

Perhaps it was the motion of the plane, the hit to the head earlier, or she was just emotionally exhausted. Either way, he had taken advantage of her nearness. He had pushed her hair out of her face, kissed her forehead, and held her hand. The man sitting on the opposite aisle in first class had eyed him, but Guy didn't care.

Lying in his bed, knowing she was just down the hall in his guest room, he couldn't sleep. He thought about Dwayne getting away, their time in the police station, and her father insisting Guy and Rori take the trip to Wyoming without him.

When Dwayne had gotten away, Guy had helped her to her feet and saw the bruise darkening on her cheek. Anger and protectiveness ruled him until the EMT on duty at the festival said she didn't have a concussion. Before today's incident, he had tried fooling himself that his protective feelings were usual for a client. But this evening, imagining her in her nightgown right down the hall from him, he knew better.

He wanted her.

Wanted her more than any other woman he had ever met. His king-sized bed seemed lonely this evening. In fact, his entire cabin seemed too big for him. He hadn't realized it until she had stepped into his kitchen, and asked, "Is this a hotel?"

Leave it to Rori to put him in his place. His cabin was too big for him, but he had started building it five years ago with the intention of sharing it…eventually.

He had always wanted children. He imagined having sons or daughters and teaching them about nature, guns, and the magazine business. He would not set his children in front of the television as a means of babysitting. He wanted any children of his to know he had time for them and loved them. With her here, he couldn't stop thinking about it.

A shuffle down the hall near the kitchen made him stop reflecting on the day's events. He threw back the sheet and green comforter and walked across the warm wood flooring to his bedroom door. Quietly, he opened the door and peeked down the hall. He saw Rori's back as she turned the corner into the kitchen. The glimpse of her had been fuzzy slippers, short blue robe, and tan bare legs.

He thought nothing of walking down the hall in his boxer shorts to see if she needed anything. When he turned the corner, he saw the freezer door open and her toned bottom sticking out. "Do you need help finding anything?"

Surprised by his voice, she hit her head on the freezer door. "Ouch! I thought you were asleep. I hope you don't mind that I helped myself."

He didn't mind at all and told her so, then added, "Nope. I even counted sheep. As much as you slept on the plane, I'm not surprised that you aren't sleeping."

"Actually, my aching head and my growling stomach won't let me. Are you hungry? I make a mean sandwich." She plopped down bread, ham, cheese, and mayo. Quick in her sandwich making, he barely had time to grab plates and glasses of water before she cut the sandwiches in two.

Sitting at his bar in their pajamas at one o'clock in the morning eating sandwiches seemed the most natural thing in the world.

He took a leap and asked a nagging question. "You seem so great at your job, I can't imagine you wanting to do anything else. What did you study at college?"

She took another bite of her sandwich and seemed to ponder his question. After swallowing, she replied, "Journalism. I wanted to be a famous journalist."

That stunned him. It was a profession so far removed gun competitions. "I'm sure you would have been a wonderful journalist. You stayed home after your mom passed, correct?"

She paled at the mention of her mom.

"I'm sorry, Rori, I'm an idiot. I shouldn't have said anything."

"No, it's fine. Really." But she remained silent as she dug into her sandwich and finished it. Guy finished his as well.

They were standing at the sink rinsing their dishes and had coffee brewing when she said, "Mom and I loved to watch movies together. She was the drama teacher at school. I worked on the school newspaper and took to interviewing the stars of the plays. Mom thought I had a knack for interviewing and writing stories for the school paper. Allowing me to go away to college and choose journalism as my major was the second time that she went against my dad's wishes."

Surprised that she was finally talking about her mom, he said the first thing he thought of. "When was the first time she went against your dad's wishes?'

Taking a sip of water, she said, "When she wouldn't let him sign me up for Glock matches when I was a teen."

"I had wondered why you didn't compete earlier." He changed the subject back to college to keep her talking. "You were thrilled to away to college, weren't you?"

"Yes. I never thought I resented my dad, but for once I didn't care about pleasing him. I wanted something for myself. Mom agreed with me. Those two years away were the best years of my life. For once, I didn't have the pressure to be my father's daughter. It was a different sort of pressure, you know? I competed with myself, not anyone else. Get better grades, write better stories, just be a better me."

"Why didn't you go back?"

She took a deep breath and exhaled. In the process, her robe shifted. He pushed the fabric back up her shoulder and handed her a cup of coffee. She took a tentative sip. "My mom passed away due to the injuries she suffered from an automobile accident. My father was driving."

"Ahh, I'm so sorry." He started to put his arm around her, but she took a step back.

"That's not all of it. He had a heart attack while he was driving. He couldn't even attend Mom's funeral because he was still in the hospital after his surgery. Then after he came home, I thought the guilt and grief would kill him. So, I stayed. I enrolled in the police academy and I'm just now looking into things *I* want to do."

"You're a good daughter. Many young girls would have left instead of staying to care for their fathers." He did hug her then, and she let him. She stared up at him. He didn't know how much more he could take before kissing her.

And that would completely blow their business relationship. They were on a fine line as it was. "Well, if you don't need anything else, I'm going to try and get some sleep."

"Sure. I thought about watching a movie, if you don't mind?"

He thought about this for a moment. He might as well enjoy her company since he wasn't going to get a wink of sleep with her down the hall. "How about I join you?"

"Sounds like a good idea."

Together they chose a Doris Day and Cary Grant movie and shared one of the big quilts draping the back of the big leather sectional sofa. Guy threw his arm around the back of the sofa. He could feel her body heat from where he sat. She was so warm, and he was hot. There wasn't a chance in hell he would fall asleep with her so close to him. But the last thing he remembered was the sound of Rori's laughter as she watched Cary and Doris tie each other in knots.

* * *

It was freaking hot. Burning up actually, something was burning like a hot furnace against her back. Rori finally remembered her surroundings. She was on Guy's couch, his legs tangled with hers, one arm around her, and she also felt something else against her back, and that made her start to get all hot bothered as well.

Breathe. Just breathe. He probably had morning happiness going on down there. Nothing to worry about. Nothing at all. Just breathe.

Rolling to her back a bit, she glanced over at Guy, who was looking straight at her.

"Good morning. Do you always look this beautiful in the morning?"

"Umm, no." Frazzled, she threw back his arm and covers, pushed her feet into her bunny slippers, and rushed down the hall to the guest room.

She could hear him calling after her, "Rori, are you alright?" No, she wasn't alright—she had major dragon breath, rats in her hair, and her legs were probably hairy by now. For the first time in years, she felt the need to primp for a man.

After a quick shower, blow dry, comb and smooth legs, she was ready to face him. Walking down the hall, she couldn't believe she had primped for him. She knew what this meant, she was falling for him. Hard, like a ton of bricks.

She reached the kitchen and smelled coffee, bacon, and something else cooking. "Are you making breakfast?"

"Yes, ma'am, I am."

She could get used to this. Waking up to a sexy man, breakfast she didn't have to drive and pick up, and coffee she didn't have to make herself. Yep, she liked this spoiled life.

He pushed coffee toward her and said, "Sit yourself down and I will fix a plate for you."

No eye contact as he said this. Umm. Maybe he thought her things to "attend" to was only an excuse to leave their growing attraction on the couch.

Once he returned to the counter with two plates, she wanted to tug him toward her. She wanted to tug him until he stood between her open legs. She wanted to reach up and pull his face down and kiss him. A slow, lingering kiss, one she hoped would make him think about something other than breakfast.

Instead, she just batted her eyes at him and said thanks.

"Eat your breakfast, young lady." He walked over to his seat, seeming unaffected by her flirting, but she smiled when she heard him mutter under his breath, "She could tempt a saint."

She dug into the awesome breakfast, feeling much better about her feminine wiles. The meal tasted like something her mom would have made her. She said it as she thought it.

Guy said, "I take that as the highest compliment," as he started on his own plate.

"So, what's on the agenda today?" Besides wanting to stay in all day and memorize every inch of his lean body.

"Well, I thought I would show you the warehouse and the magazine shop. It is all housed on the same campus, but we have to maintain separate buildings for the equipment."

She thought about that for a moment as she took a long drink of cold orange juice. "How many buildings are there?"

He answered her question with much detail and enthusiasm. "There are three. One for the magazine, with room for photo shoots, and working cubicles. One for the test facility, which has its own built-in range, and then the last building is the warehouse, which houses the entire inventory. Three buildings are enough for now, but we would also like to print the magazine here in Jackson one day. Currently, it is put out by the print shop in Cheyenne."

She thought that over. "Isn't that the southeastern point of Wyoming? It seems like it would be easier for you to have all of the magazine operation here."

He nodded. "It would be, but the previous owner of the magazine lived in Cheyenne. The publishing jobs have always been in Cheyenne. The employees would either have to move here or find other jobs. It isn't possible for SG to pay for moving expenses."

"Isn't the magazine successful?"

"Yes, it has always been successful, but we can't take on a move like that at this point in time. Our success is due to the employees. I don't want to mess with any jobs until I can find a clean way to move the printing process. A fair way."

"Sounds like quite a setup. So, how many people do you employ?"

"Two hundred year-round, but the number grows to about three hundred during Christmas time."

"Wow, I never thought about all that. You have quite a bit of responsibility, don't you?"

She admired him beyond the point of adoration. Not only was he hot, smart, and funny, but he was kind as well. The man made her heart thump loudly.

Instead of throwing herself at him as she had wanted to do from the moment she woke up this morning, she stood, left her napkin on her plate, and offered to clean up.

"Thanks, but you are a guest. Why don't you take your coffee and go sit on the deck?" He tossed her a jacket and said, "I'll come get you when I'm ready."

The view was unlike any she had ever witnessed, she thought, as she sat in one of the wooden deck chairs on the wrap-around porch. The mountains, the colorful trees, the peace and quiet. Breathtaking. And cold! She had never been so cold in July. She pulled her bare legs up under her and covered them with Guy's big jacket. It was barely nine o'clock, and it would warm up as the day progressed.

Sipping her coffee, taking in the view, she thought back to the events of the past few days.

Unbelievable.

Definitely something out of a Lifetime movie, one minute she had been going about her business and the next she met Mr.

Perfect and was accused of abducting Mr. Crazy, the latter turning out to not have disappeared at all.

She was sure that her dad and all his techy know-how would find a trail if Dwayne had left one. How were his parents taking the news that their son was on the path to crazy? Surely, they had an idea that their only child had been capable of dubious things such as faking his own disappearance.

But why? The only thing she could think of was that seeing her with Guy had lit some sort of fuse with Dwayne. That night at the Pizza Grill had been the last straw for her. Apparently, it had been the last straw for Dwayne as well. She wished she could turn back the clock and take back her actions. She had just been so frustrated, and she had acted impulsively by dumping that beer on him.

The only good to come of this was that Dwayne was off the force. Finally, she could work in peace. Go about her life without interference from him.

*Geez.* Time to shake that off. It would all work out.

While she was here, Rori planned on learning as much as she could from Guy and to just enjoy his company.

There were worse things than spending time with the man she was falling in love with.

# CHAPTER SIX

He didn't know how it happened, but his nice, quiet day with Rori had turned into a shooting competition between Rori and Brock.

His test facility in Jackson had a separate indoor range, and it was currently in use by the two most competitive people he knew. His best friend and his...Rori.

Not sure how to label their relationship, Guy had almost forgotten about the stupid contract until she had mentioned it to Brock. So, now Brock thought his relationship with her was only professional, and he had to deal with Brock hitting on her for the better part of the day. The sound of her laugh usually filled him with heat, but hearing it in response to Brock's stupid jokes made him sick to his stomach.

Why hadn't he said something to show Brock he intended to...intended to what? He wasn't sure. Her laughter and Brock's growing list of witty lines grated his nerves. It helped that she was beating the pants off his friend. Since they had grown up together, he knew Brock was as turned on by her skill as he had been. He clenched his hand into a fist as he watched Brock touch her arm…and watched her smile in return.

Luck was not on his side today.

Never did he think Brock would stop by for a visit. Sure, he stopped by regularly during the week. Usually, he and Brock would test out new equipment, or Brock would just use the range. But, today of all days, Guy just flat out didn't want him around.

Watching Rori now, he realized he needed to seal the deal with her. Both professionally and personally before Brock had any wise-guy ideas. He knew actions spoke louder than words, but he just didn't know how to approach her. *Hell.* He was thinking like a damned teenager.

Tired of his current nonchalant stance, Guy removed his hands from his jeans pockets and crossed his arms over his chest. He stared through the bulletproof glass and saw Brock move behind Rori, just imagining his friend inhaling her coconut-scented hair. Don Juan was probably drooling now. She was dressed in her typical outfit of boots, shorts, and tank top that really showed off her perfect, tanned skin. When she focused on her targets, she did this little twitch with her ponytail. Long, blond hair brushing against her shoulders caught the attention of any man in her vicinity.

Lord, he wanted her. He hadn't felt this jealous since he and Brock had almost argued over taking Melanie Milsap to the senior prom. It ended up that neither one of them had taken

Melanie since they realized she had played both of them. After they figured it out, they each wrote her notes during school asking her to meet them, at different times of course. Brock's meeting with Melanie occurred right after school. Little did Melanie know, Guy was hidden under the bleachers while she pawed all over Brock. The same happened thirty minutes later when Guy saw her at the roller rink. Brock learned Melanie was a player, just like him. They decided she must have a perverse need to come between two best friends. It didn't happen. He and Brock decided way back then a woman would never come between them.

It had worked out then and it would work out now. But Rori wasn't just *any* woman. Guy needed to let his friend know, subtly, that she would never be part of his growing list of girlfriends.

Plus, Brock pictured himself the ultimate ladies' man. For the most part, that image of himself and his prowess with the ladies was correct. Women loved him, always had, and his many broken engagements were proof he loved them right back. At this point, the guy should get a discount on engagement rings from the jewelry store in town.

Back in high school, Brock and Guy hadn't argued over Melanie, but he sure would fight over Aurora Cross.

Forget the bro code.

He wanted to forget the bro code. *But* dudes kept to the code. It was unspoken. He and Brock had followed the code with Melanie—neither one of them had dated her. Their friendship had been more important.

What did this say about his growing feelings for Rori if Guy was ready to rip his best friend from limb to limb for smelling her hair? Was he losing it, or was she really the one?

He thought she might be the woman for him. The tour of the SG facilities today had been for the sole purpose of showing her his world in the hopes it world would become part of her world. Today he had wanted her to see what life would encompass if she chose to sign the contract, and also if their professional relationship grew into something personal.

Although they had only shared a few days together, he didn't feel he was jumping the gun. The flicker in her eyes when she looked at him, her soft murmur as she said his name. He wasn't imagining it. Was he? He thought she felt the same way.

The short amount of time they had known each other seemed like much longer than just a few days. He couldn't imagine being separated from her. Not even for a day. The fact she had a life back in Ohio didn't matter. Somehow they would make it work. All that mattered was this feeling between them, and at the present moment, getting rid of his best friend.

Brock and Rori had finished shooting their targets and were carrying them over to him.

"Check this out, Guy. I beat Brock. Are you sure he practices as much as you think he does?" Her grin was full of mischief as she proudly displayed her cardboard targets for Guy's inspection.

"According to Brock, he practices daily."

Brock threw back his head and laughed. His dark blond hair had been lightened by the summer sun. Though he was much shorter than Guy, he seemed the perfect height for Rori. She only had to look up a bit to him. Brock was in his work uniform of green pants, button-up shirt, steel-toed boots, with Rori in her boots and shorts. The two of them standing so close together, and looking like the perfect soap opera couple, went right through him.

"Guy, you know, as the game warden I have to be ready for anything. But I could practice twenty-four-seven, and this pretty little lady would still have the advantage on me. You picked a good one, I'll give you that."

When he said "pretty little lady" she blushed a little. So, she wasn't unaffected by him. This could be a problem. Well, Guy would just have to just have to keep his friend away while she was here. And he planned on keeping Rori so busy she wouldn't have any time to spend with anyone but him.

Guy stared at Rori until she looked down at her toes. Had he just caught her fantasizing about his best friend? Was that the reason she looked away?

"Do you have plans for this evening?" Brock spoke in his come-hither voice directed at Rori.

"No, why?" she asked casually and threw a quick glance at Guy.

He had to step in. "Actually, I'm taking Rori out to dinner. We have work stuff to discuss." He thought his response would stop Brock in his tracks, but he was wrong.

"Well, there is a concert tonight, a tribute band playing in Jackson. Maybe after your dinner, the two of you could come join me."

He just bet Brock wanted him there, but no way would he leave them alone. "Sure, sounds like a plan."

His friend was watching him intently. "Great, man. See you

both at eight o'clock. Rori, it was a pleasure to meet such a pretty, talented lady." He kissed the back of her hand.

He watched Brock go out the door and started sweeping up brass furiously. He felt Rori stare into his back. The thought of those lips touching her sent the broom flying faster across the floor. Brass went all directions except the dustpan.

She sidestepped some of it and asked, "Guy? Are you mad at me about something?"

Her sweet voice sounded hurt, and he couldn't hold in his anger in any longer. Still sweeping, he didn't look up as he replied. "No. But I'm mad at Brock. He has always been too slick for his own good."

"So, are you jealous?"

"No, I just need you focused on what we are doing here. You have no time to play with Brock."

She threw her head back and laughed. "Whatever you say, Mr. Editor."

Guy scowled at her, and she laughed even harder. Walking over to him she stood so close, close enough to kiss, but she took the broom from him and started sweeping.

"You have nothing to worry about. I am always focused and professional. I've been around jocks like Brock my entire life, and I find his type amusing."

"You do?"

"Yes, I do."

She leaned on the broom and looked at him hard. The smell of gunpowder on her hands mixed with her coconut scent made him want to kiss her. He wanted to push her shirt up and feel her warm skin, pull her tight against him, and just devour her.

They were so intent on staring at each other that neither heard his receptionist, Lucy, come into the room. Clearing her throat, Lucy said, "Excuse me, Mr. Matthews, Miss Cross, but there is a call for Mr. Matthews on line one."

Lucy had just graduated from the vocational school, and although she was young, she was turning into a fine receptionist. She blushed, and he wanted to groan for thinking about putting his hands up a client's shirt.

Damn, his thoughts were in the gutter, and his professionalism was going out the window. He was no better than a high school boy.

"Thank you, Lucy, but please take a message." His statement and his tone were a warning to her not to interrupt him when he was with a client.

"But it is a member of the board. That's why I interrupted…" Lucy had been told on her first day of work that whenever a board member called, she was to locate Guy and tell him immediately. Unfortunately, today was not a good day for a board member phone call.

Rori had yet to sign the contract. If he looked as if he dreaded the phone call as much as he felt it, he didn't blame Lucy for hightailing it out of the room.

Rori had started sweeping up the rest of the brass during his conversation with Lucy, but she stopped when they were alone again. "I forgot to mention, I've decided to sign the contract. A few needed stipulations, but I'll sign it after those changes are made."

"What are your stipulations?" He hoped his question sounded calm and cool, not like the panic it sounded to his ears.

"Well, the two major ones are: I set my own competition schedule and I write my own articles. You get those two approved, and we can compromise on the third I have in mind." She looked everywhere except directly at him.

Didn't she know that he would move mountains for her?

He had to remember this was a business deal first, so he put on a mask of indifference, and in his brisk professional voice replied, "That is doable. I need to go take this call. You can come with me or practice some more."

She straightened her back a bit, surprised by his tone. "I will practice more. You go face the music."

He wasn't surprised that she opted to practice. She didn't need more practice today, but she probably knew he was requesting privacy for this phone call.

This call was important, but not as important as her feelings. Once this call was over and the contract signed, he would be able to breathe and could sort out any hurt feelings by his abruptness.

Man, it took a long time to go over the contract line by line, but Guy had wanted her to do so before signing it.

Rori was now an official spokesperson for SG magazine. Her first cover shoot was scheduled in a couple days, and that issue would come out in a few months.

There were also several matches throughout the year where she would represent SG magazine, wearing their gear and demonstrating their customized guns. She knew this was a good leap, but she also had one more request.

The last minor request had been a small detail to Guy. She wanted to style her own photo shoots. He had approved, and she had signed on the dotted line. She had seen some of the other magazine covers with female models on them and she detested them. This last request would ensure she didn't join the leagues of those models wearing too little clothing and too much makeup.

After almost fifteen years of buying her own magazines from the range, Rori knew what direction she wanted her photo shoot to go. Nothing sleazy, and it had to be very informative to women and men as well. Women had come a long way in gun sports, but there were still those magazines with covers of women holding rifles wearing bikinis.

*Disgusting.*

Good thing Guy felt the same way, or appeared to, since he agreed to all her demands. He was currently talking on the phone, discussing the signed contract and the upcoming photo shoot, while she practiced in the indoor range.

The SG indoor range was one of the best she had ever been in. State-of-the-art electronic equipment, great lighting, and a viewing room. Three rounds of targets and she was going strong. She did her best thinking at the range. The action of shooting was so automatic to her, she could probably do it in the dark with one arm behind her back.

Behind her back? She had never practiced trick shooting before. What great idea for an article.

When she had requested to write her own articles, Guy

hadn't batted an eye. It was almost as if he knew her so well already he anticipated her mind would go in that direction. She still hadn't told him about the class she wanted to take, but she would soon.

He thought writing the articles herself was an excellent idea. He had even laughed and said it would save him money. Even though he had never read anything she had ever written, he was willing to put his neck on the line and vouch for her.

*What if she sucked?*

She brushed the thought aside. The last few days might have zapped her confidence, but her track record rocked. The only thing she couldn't do well was cook. Yep. She truly bombed in the kitchen.

Putting down her Glock and removing the last magazine, she thought that her dream of becoming a journalist may not have happened the way she had planned, but it seemed she was on her way to having her own by-line.

Would her mom have been proud? Rori hoped so. Her father, on the other hand, wasn't going to be happy. She could hear him now, *"What about the NBPD?"* It had always been the police force with Edward. The one bone of contention with her father was her job. Rori was a good policewoman, but it was a job to her. Not a vocation. She wanted something that would drive her, not drive her crazy.

Police work was hard. Not that she sidestepped hard work, but the crazy hours, violent crimes, and the children she had to escort to Children's Services on a weekly basis…well, it sucked. These were just a few of the reasons her job had become just a job. She was tired. Tired of not having control of her own life.

Her job was her father's dream, not hers.

She may not have her dream of becoming a famous journalist, but representing SG magazine, competing, traveling, writing, and spending time with Guy was darn close.

Just thinking of the sexy man, and poof, he entered the indoor range where she had just started sweeping the rest of the brass from her third practice session with his Glock 19. He must have finished his second call to the board member. He was grinning, a good sign her demands hadn't created any ripples.

"Well?" she demanded as she leaned on the long-handled broom.

"Well, they said if you can write an article as well-executed as you shoot a gun, they will be happy campers. I told them I was betting my money on you."

"Ha! You aren't betting anything. I think you plan on the details, Guy." She bent down and picked up the dustpan full of brass and dumped it in a plastic tub for re-loading.

"Maybe, but I believe in your ability to conquer anything."

She turned and looked at him, *really* looked at him. "Thank you. Thank you for all of this."

She would have never thought it possible, but he seemed to blush at her words of gratitude. "I really mean it, Guy. You have no idea what this opportunity means to me. Now, all that's left is to tell my father."

He moved closer and took the broom out of her hands, then put his hands on her shoulders. "I think I do. And when you get around to telling your father you signed the contract, we'll do it together."

# CHAPTER SEVEN

*W*e'll do it together.

Rori had contemplated Guy's words for the rest of the day. She had thought about it during their leisurely lunch in the town square, a hike along the hills behind his log cabin, and now on their way to the concert.

She liked the way *we* had flowed from his lips so easily. Neither one of them had exactly spoken out loud what she was sure they were both thinking.

In the span of the week, two individuals were becoming a *we*. They would be a couple that said things like, *we don't know what we are doing this weekend* or *we would love to meet you for coffee.*

So far, she thought she liked this *we* stuff. A true romantic at heart, she imagined Guy professing his undying love for her. Hopefully not in John Deere green on the water tower, but something romantic.

Something memorable.

Something to repeat to her kids and grandkids. Maybe a whisper of love in her ear on top of the Empire State Building? Or maybe he would shout out his love for her while on horse-back on an exotic beach somewhere?

Yes, she had watched too many romantic comedies, but darn it, why shouldn't she have the fairy tale? Why couldn't she have a Prince Charming with the happily ever after?

The man who consumed most of her thoughts nowadays broke the comfortable silence. "Did you know Brock and I were once in a band?"

Not expecting that at all, she laughed. "What kind of band? No, wait. Let me guess…you two were in a country band. That's what y'all listen to out here, right?"

"No, for your information neither of us like country music. In fact, neither one of us can sing or play an instrument."

Befuddled over his last statement, Rori said, "Then how were you both in a band?"

"Have you ever heard of air guitar?"

He explained the many high school talent shows the two won lip-synching and playing the air guitar and air drums.

"Guy, that is unlike any high school talent show I have ever heard of."

"Brock's sister, Brianne, and his mom always filmed the talent shows. I'm sure if you wanted to watch a few, you could."

She laughed again. "I'd like nothing more than to see you lip-synch." She wanted to know all about Guy—his family, his friends, even sit through his home videos.

He pulled his black Chevy Tahoe into the parking lot of the

civic arena. "I'm sure this concert will be excellent. The arena has new sound equipment, and the seats are comfortable."

"I don't care about the seats, as I usually stand during concerts."

"Oh, no, you aren't one of those standing screamers, are you?"

"Only when necessary." She blushed as she realized her comment could be taken another way.

"Is that another blush, Miss Cross?" Guy asked, amused. She shook her head no.

"No, the heated seats in this honking SUV are getting to me." She knew the heated seats weren't turned on, but he kindly let her comment slide.

He pulled into a parking spot and put the SUV into park. Unbuckling his belt, he said, "Stay right there. I'm going to come around and help you down. No, no, don't argue, I insist on opening the door for you."

He opened the car door and rushed around the front of his vehicle, then opened the door for her. She smiled down at him as he helped her down.

"What?"

"Nothing, I just thought how wonderful it is to be with a gentleman. I don't think any man has ever demanded I stay put so he can open my door. You are one of a kind, Mr. Matthews."

He still had her in his arms and hadn't yet released her when someone yelled, "I hate public displays of affection!" This came from a high-pitched voice coming toward them across the lot.

A short redhead approached them. She was smiling and

waved to Guy. This woman was decked out in black leather boots, short denim shorts, a leather vest, and tons of jewelry.

Rori felt underdressed in her casual sandals, black capris, and tank top. She had followed Guy's lead when picking out her outfit this evening. He had finished getting ready before she had, and she had gotten a glimpse of his khaki pants and t-shirt. He had informed her they were going to a barbeque restaurant, good food, but very laid-back atmosphere. Apparently, they needed to change into leather for the concert.

"Brianne Rose, I didn't know you would be here. Brock should've told me, we would have picked you up." Guy had dropped Rori to her feet and was giving this Brianne a big hug when Rori cleared her throat.

Guy seemed to remember his manners and introduced them. "Brianne Walker, meet Aurora Cross. Rori is SG's new spokesperson and came all the way from Ohio. Rori, Bri is Brock's little sister, and my adopted little sister."

Brianne stuck her hand out to shake Rori's. "Call me Bri. New spokesperson? Looks to me like your new girlfriend by the heavy petting I just witnessed."

Rori didn't know what to say but didn't have a chance since Brianne started questioning her. "So, Aurora, did your mother name you after Sleeping Beauty?"

Her stunned expression must have given her away as she answered, unsure of where this line of questioning would lead. "Umm, yes, but not many people make the connection."

Guy laughed and interjected, "Well, you are looking at Briar Rose."

Brianne slapped him hard on the arm. He didn't even flinch. "Guy, let me tell the story. It *is* about *me* after all."

Brianne slipped her arm through Rori's and started walking toward the civic arena. She related the story of how her mother named her Briar Rose after Sleeping Beauty.

"My dad and Brock refused to call me by my given name and nicknamed me Brianne. I never officially changed my name, so on paper I'm still Briar Rose. My mother loves the name so much, and that has been the only thing stopping me from officially changing my name."

Not skipping a beat, she continued her tale, "I'd been teased the first week of school when the teacher would call out my name. I'd ask to be called, Brianne but sometimes my teacher would refuse."

Her story finished by the time the three of them walked across the parking lot to the arena doors. *Whew!* Bri could talk. Rori wondered if she had been a spitfire even as a child.

Once inside at the ticket window, Brianne yelled to Guy, "Hey, big brother. Be a doll and pay, would ya?" She giggled, and Rori smiled.

"Of course, Brianne. Don't I always?" He got in front of them and bought both their tickets.

Rori murmured her thanks, but Brianne just smiled sweetly as if she deserved everything Guy could provide for her.

She listened closely as Guy lowered his voice. "Brianne, it is unlike you to come alone. Who's meeting you here?"

Brianne bristled at his words. "Guy, you are such a downer. Why do you think I have to be meeting someone?"

Rori dropped her arm from Brianne's and took a few steps

back to give the two some room for a private conversation, but she couldn't help but hear Guy's words as he raised his voice a level.

"Let me guess. You didn't find a date in time. Even with all the names in your little black book, so you are waiting on Tucker."

Brianne's freckles seemed to grow together as her face went hot. "Tuck will be here after he finishes his last class. Plus, my relationship with him is none of your business."

"Brianne…" Guy started to lecture his adopted baby sister, but then Brock came in the door. He was alone, and Guy didn't look too pleased to see him.

Brock walked right over to Rori to say hello. She could smell his aftershave. It was a pleasant musky scent, but nothing as sexy as Guy's. "Hi, Brock. Thanks again for inviting us to the concert. I'm looking forward to it."

Guy moved away from Brianne and put his arm around Rori's waist. No, he definitely was not happy that Brock was dateless. "Brock, I assume you already have a ticket since you knew about this concert to begin with."

"You are right on, my friend. So, would you little ladies like some snacks before the concert?"

Rori caught the undercurrent going on. "Guy already took me for a nice dinner, but thank you for asking, Brock."

Brianne snickered. "Guy, this one is so polite." Then to Brock she said, "You can get me a drink and some nachos. And I don't have to say thanks, do I? You know I appreciate you, Brockie."

Brock surprised Rori by hugging Brianne and murmuring,

"Anything for my little sis." She had expected Brock to tease Brianne in some way—at least that was what she thought big brothers did. She never anticipated the sensitivity Brock displayed. She wondered what he was hiding behind his womanizer persona.

* * *

Man, this blew. Seriously.

The music was great, and so was Guy's company, but Rori was in a pickle. Brianne kept telling off the complete strangers making out right beside her. Sure, the noises coming from the couple were louder than the band, but Brianne was even more distracting. Rori had heard some rough language, but never from a five-foot-nothing woman. Brianne thought she was six feet tall and bulletproof.

So far, Rori had refrained from reining the other woman in. For crying out loud, she had just met her thirty minutes ago and she shouldn't have to put on her police hat.

*Crap.* She hated to put Brianne in her place.

The guys had gone to grab some drinks and concert t-shirts, so she was on her own with Brianne. The couple next to Bri were making out as if it was their last night together. And they were darn tipsy. Sure, it wasn't the place for such a make-out session, but there were worse things than having your evening ruined at a twenty-dollar concert.

Rori had handled tipsy before. What she couldn't handle was Brianne.

Bri exacerbated the situation. Her anger was uncalled for, and she continued to raise her voice.

"You assholes need to get a room and go screw until you both can't see straight. Stupid morons!"

Was this the type of behavior that Guy had been about to lecture her on before Brock arrived? And who was this Tucker person that he had mentioned?

Either Brianne craved attention, or she had major anger issues.

Rori realized the face-sucking going on was enough to make everyone around them uncomfortable too, but geez, ignore it, and watch the concert.

She had to step in before the couple retaliated against Brianne's anger. Guy had never really talked about Brianne, and Rori didn't have a good feel for her. Sighing, she put on her policewoman hat and did what she would've done had it been anyone else. She tapped Bri on the shoulder. "Brianne, you are really disturbing the others around you. Please knock it off, or I am going to take you outside to cool off."

"Me? Are you kidding? Romeo and Juliet here are the problem. I'm just voicing what everyone else is thinking. No one else has the balls to do it." She tossed her red hair back and gave Romeo and Juliet another rant.

"Brianne!"

Rori had been expecting Brock or Guy, but a tall, blond stranger came barreling down the stadium stairs. "Brianne, what are you doing?"

Bri froze for just a second, and then turned her attention to the newcomer. Rori watched in fascination as her fury went up another notch. "Well, Tucker, as you can see... I was telling the trash to get a room. I had to take care of it myself since you never seem to show up in time for anything!"

Brock and Guy came down the stairs right as drunken Romeo decided he wanted to start something. Brianne tried to take control and slap his hand away, but Tucker acted quickly and removed her from harm's way.

Before Rori knew what had happened, Guy and Brock had taken care of Romeo, and Tucker had bundled Brianne up and was carrying her up the stairs.

Rori dared to lean into Guy and whisper, "What the hell was that all about?"

"Later. I'll tell you later. Let's just enjoy the rest of the concert."

So, she did. The remainder of the concert was better. Romeo and Juliet had cooled it, and Guy had wrapped his arm around her shoulder. They sang along with the band. There weren't too many songs that she didn't know, but Guy knew them all.

Either he had heard this band before, or the age difference had given him a one up on her. She didn't mind.

At one point, Brock and Guy played their air guitars. Two grown men should have been embarrassed, she thought. They weren't, though. She smiled as she watched their shameless antics.

Looking at Guy, she knew how she wanted this night to end...with her arms wrapped around him.

Guy tried to take his own advice and enjoy the rest of the concert, but he was still thinking of Brianne and the tangle she had almost caused. Tiny, redheaded, and freckled. She had been teased by everyone growing up. Unlike Rori, who seemed to excel at everything she put her mind to, Bri had to practice, practice, and practice yet again.

Brianne currently worked in a gun shop and taught classes on proper gun safety. This career had been a long time coming for her, and Guy, as her adopted brother, was so relieved she had finally figured out her professional life. Now, if she could figure out the personal side, he and Brock would have many more sleep-filled nights.

Overall, this hadn't turned out to be his night. He had imagined this night to be special. He had wanted to cross the line, no, jump over the line. He had wanted to stand behind Rori, hug her in a cheesy sort of way. They would sway to the music, pull out lighters or hold up cell phones. He hadn't thought her attention would be monopolized by his friends.

Brianne wanting to talk about Sleeping Beauty and started a fight, and then Brock tried his own cheesy moves on Rori, offering her drinks, snacks, and a concert t-shirt. No—not the night he had planned.

He thought negatively about this for a few seconds more, and then let it go. Rori was interesting. He wanted to know more about her, so why wouldn't he expect his closest friends wouldn't want to do the same?

Also, if Rori could get Brianne's attention, and that was a magical feat, then her SG magazine cover coming out in a couple of months would capture the attention of even the pickiest audience.

So, instead of getting all jealous of his friends, Guy appreciated the feeling on both a personal level and a professional level.

With positive thoughts, he stood with his arm across her shoulder and swayed back and forth to the music.

# CHAPTER EIGHT

The night had been full of crazy, but it also had its nice moments. Extremely tired and a bit confused, Rori couldn't stop her head dipping down to rest on her right shoulder. She figured she was still a little jet-lagged.

She would just close her eyes a bit, and Guy would wake her when they arrived back at his house. There was the feeling of being lifted in the air, and she knew Guy was carrying her. So darn sleepy, why couldn't she wake up? She tried to communicate that to him, but he said, "I know, sweetheart, and it has been a long week for you."

She snuggled in closer and only felt a moment of guilt before she was dead to the world. She liked him calling her sweetheart.

She woke up the next morning in a haze in Guy's guest room. Her stomach rolled, and she made a quick dash to the connecting bathroom. After losing her stomach, she thought back to the previous night and realized that she still had on her capris and tank. Guy, gentleman that he was, had helped her to bed, removed her shoes, and covered her with the comforter.

After taking a shower, quick because she couldn't stand very long due to weak knees, she had to face the facts. She was sick. She couldn't remember the last time she had been sick. Maybe it would pass in a bit. Snug in her blue robe, she lay on top of the bed with her hair still wrapped in a towel. She planned to get up in a few minutes and get dressed. She just needed to rest a few more minutes before going in search of Guy.

Guy started to worry about Rori. It was past nine, and she hadn't appeared for coffee yet. He thought he had heard her start the shower. What if she had fallen? Creeping down the hall, he peaked in the guest room door. "Rori?"

Opening the door wider, he saw her sprawled across the bed, asleep and wearing only her blue robe. Approaching her, he pushed back a strand of long, blond hair that had escaped her towel. In the process, he brushed her forehead. She was burning up.

Worried, he tried to wake her. "Rori, please wake up."

Mumbling, she rolled over, giving Guy a glimpse of one pale breast. With a shaking hand, he reached down and covered her up. "Rori, I think you have a high temperature. Do you feel ill?"

She managed to nod, then muttered, "Already been sick this morning."

"Here, sit up, and I will help you under the covers. Then, I am going to find a thermometer."

Rushing to the kitchen to find his first aid kit, he found the thermometer in the same location. He also grabbed some stomachache medicine and aspirin, not knowing what could help her.

Propped up against the large pillows and barely awake, she looked tiny and pitiful. And adorable. Even sick, she made him think inappropriate thoughts. "Open your mouth put this under your tongue." She was unable to do as he instructed, so he replied said, "Well, I will hold it for you."

This was not part of the plan. He had intended on getting her ready for the photo shoot in two days. Instead, here she was unable to hold her head up, and he worried that her fever would get worse. Looking down at his watch he realized it was time to check the thermometer. Damn, her temperature was over one hundred. "I'm calling the doctor."

He rushed to the phone like he had a fire under his feet. His nearest neighbor was a doctor and wouldn't mind a trip out. The doctor should be home, if not, Guy was screwed. The nearest hospital was twenty-five miles away, and he worried that he would be unable to drive and assist Rori if she were sick. He could lay her down in the back seat of the Tahoe, but if she was sick again, he didn't want to worry about her airway being free.

Damn. His neighbor, Harold, wasn't answering his house phone. He tried the good doctor's cell phone. Success.

Some twenty minutes later, the doctor arrived and checked Rori over, declaring it was nothing more than a nasty bug. The doctor ordered plenty of fluids, medicine, and two days of bed rest.

So relieved, Guy sat down beside Rori and just watched her. She had fallen asleep as soon as the doctor had stopped poking and prodding her. The doctor had warned that she may be sick again during the night, so Guy planned to be right here for her.

A long afternoon of busy work went by with him checking in on her often. She had awoken several times during the afternoon, and he had helped her to the bathroom. She had needed help sitting up and walking to the bathroom, but she had firmly shut the door in his face each time. So, that meant she was getting better. He would be really worried about her if she was too sick to care if he saw her helpless.

It was now nightfall, and he rested in the guest chair in her room and watched her.

She stirred, opened her eyes, and saw him. She was a bit pale, her hair looked like a lioness, and he still thought she looked lovely. His heart was in deep trouble around her. "Good. You are awake. Are you hungry? Thirsty?"

"You don't have to be my nurse. I'm fine," she said as she managed to sit up by herself.

"Rori, you have been in this bed for twenty-four hours straight. You are not fine."

She shrugged her shoulders, but not before he caught the evil-eye she gave him. "You look terrible, go shower and change before I start feeling guilty."

Good, she felt well enough to sass him. "Fine, but after that, I will be right back with some supper."

He returned with food, a deck of cards, and a laptop. She had changed her pajamas and combed her hair while he had been away. "I thought after some soup you could try to beat me in rummy."

In the short time he had known Rori, he knew she never backed down from a challenge. "You're on, Mr. Editor." She paused and looked at the laptop. "What's the laptop for?"

"I thought you could spend the rest of your time in quarantine writing."

Hesitating a bit, he added, "I also have a message from your father."

"About Dwayne?" she asked.

"Yes."

She digested that information for a minute. "Did they find him yet?"

"No, they haven't. If you don't feel like calling Edward back, I'll do it." He felt the need to reach out to Edward, as he was probably the most taciturn person he had ever met.

She smiled and murmured her thanks.

Her smile melted his heart. Guy placed the supper tray in the middle of the bed. He climbed in on the other side and took a cup of tea and a cup of soup for himself and placed them on the side table. He then moved the tray onto her lap. Using his best British accent, "My lady, your dinner: a fine chicken broth, applesauce, crackers, and tea. Do you require anything else?"

"Yes, food."

The twinkle in her eye told him she teased, but he felt the need to add, "Harold prescribed this diet until your stomach isn't in knots. Wait until you see what we are having for breakfast tomorrow."

She giggled. "Your British accent is horrible."

Damn, he was still using the accent. "Bloody hell."

That statement caused her to laugh until she noticed her cup of tea sliding toward the end of the tray.

"I think you may be the only man I know capable of knowing how to curse in different accents."

They spent the rest of the evening with Guy doing his best accents and making up curse words. They played rummy, and Rori, of course, beat him. She seemed to be feeling better, but he didn't want to tire her out. Gathering up the cards, he tucked them into his front pocket. Then he checked her forehead one last time with the back of his hand and said, "I'm going to head into my office for a while. If you need anything, just yell."

"I will. Thank you."

As he left the room, he watched her pick up the laptop and stare as if it was a foreign object. He hoped she would find her voice for the articles and that he wasn't expecting too much from her. He knew she excelled in just about everything she set her mind to, but it had been four years since she had attended college. And if she hadn't written anything since college, he trusted she could just get back on the bike and blow her first article out of the water. The last two days being cooped up had probably given her time to sort things out and develop a strategy. If this turned out to be successful, SG magazine might want her on a full-time basis. But he wasn't ready to put that kind of pressure on her.

Reflecting, he headed down to his den, which also served as his home office. He loved this room. Wooden benches sat next to the tall bookcases where sometimes he would start a fire and sit down with a good book. But most of the time, he used it for working, which he did have plenty to do today after playing nurse to Rori.

He picked up the phone and returned Edward's call. One to get the update on Dwayne, and two, he intended to ask his daughter on a date and he felt he should ask his permission. As scared as Guy was at Edward's response, he wanted Rori more.

\* \* \*

Rori spent two days recovering in Guy's guest bedroom writing articles, basically blog entries, and watching old movies. Almost a mini-vacation, except for being ill most of yesterday, and she'd enjoyed Guy's pampering and was delighted with the work she had produced.

It had been so long since she had written anything, but it felt like…home. The feeling compared to the rightness of working on the high school paper and assisting her mom. Almost like the adrenaline rush when she shot her Glock. But a different type of rush. It was hard to describe it, but she just knew that writing the last couple of days had given her a release.

Release from the stress she had been holding on to.

The stress from her mom's passing, giving up college, caring for her dad, demands of work, Dwayne. All of it had lifted during the last days writing in isolation.

What a relief to finally live her life as she wanted. That thought brought a bit of guilt with it. Her dad would be lonely, and she hoped he wouldn't fall in the hole she had found him in after her mom's death.

Guy had intercepted her calls from her father while she was

ill, and she had let the others and unknown calls go to voice-mail. It wasn't until this morning that she and Guy had told Edward about signing the contract and the photo shoot.

Her father hadn't been as upset as she thought he would be. Of course, he had been concerned that she was ill and he thanked Guy for taking care of her.

Edward also had some news for them. He had been suspicious that Dwayne always knew where to find Rori. Sure enough, his suspicions were confirmed when he found a tracking device under her truck.

Edward was working on the device now and he hoped to locate Dwayne. He seemed surprised by Dwayne's ease with technology. This knowledge and Dwayne's deviousness scared Rori.

Guy popped his head in her door. "Feeling better?"

"Much better, Mr. Editor, come on in. I have something for you to read."

Feeling nauseous, and not due to her recent illness, she pushed the open laptop across the bed to him. He had taken up the habit of sitting on the other side of the bed when he came in each time to check on her.

She had written the backstory for the article that would accompany her first cover. She watched Guy's expression as he read with her heart in her throat. "Well?"

He sat back against the extra set of pillows. He seemed to be measuring his words. "Rori, this is good. I mean, better than good. Your mother was right to have sided with you when you went away to college."

She almost cried at his words of praise. Almost. "Thank you.

I've been saving up for an online course I wanted to take this fall."

He looked into her eyes for a long time. "You are welcome, and I think that is great that you want to take an online course. SG can pay for the course as part of your next contract."

Taking the computer back from him, she continued with her ideas for future projects. "Thanks, but I have it covered. I think my articles should all be in diary format. So, as soon as the shoot is over tomorrow, I want to capture my thoughts. May I use this laptop tomorrow?"

"Keep it. It is an extra the magazine had laying around, and I brought it home a month or so ago."

She smiled her thanks and continued to look at the screen. Her hands flew across the keyboard as her mind went into overdrive, and she was in a hurry to get around to the next bend.

"For someone not into computers, you seem to know your way around one."

Pausing in her speed-typing, she shrugged. "I'm average at computers. I'm not at my dad's level, so that means I'm just good. You wouldn't believe the things my dad can find. I couldn't get away with anything as a child. Not even downloading songs without his permission."

He threw back his head and laughed. "What kind of songs would you download?"

"Oh, you know, rock-n-roll…Edward hates it."

He stood to leave. "Well, rock goddess, get ready. We need to be in Jackson in two hours. Do you need any help with your shower?" He grinned at his question.

Throwing a pillow at him, she said, "No, now get out."

She didn't think any woman would want help in the shower by a sexy man after being sick. The only time she wanted his shower assistance was if he was in there with her.

It was a shame that he was putting business first. Even though he had stayed right by her side, nursing her back to health, and had flirted about helping her in the shower, it was all business.

He needed her but not in the romantic sense. She was not going to make the first move. She was gun shy.

Yes, gun shy.

After the spell with her college boyfriend, she hadn't allowed herself to have a serious relationship since. Not that the college guy had lasted very long, but she had thought she was in love with him. How young and dumb she had been.

Had that only been a little over four years ago? She had tried to give herself a little credit for her huge misjudgment of character. It had been the first time she had been away from home, she had never had a boyfriend, and she let a few nice compliments and common interests distract her from what a pig he had been.

Nope. With her mind made up, she wasn't about to make a jerk of herself and force herself on Guy Matthews.

No way was she leading this game. The ball was now firmly in his court. He could continue with his little flirting lines and the deep stares and all that. She would not cave, he would have to make the first move.

Oh, she hoped that he would, and soon. He was her dream man. He just needed a push.

Throwing her lethargic legs over the side of the bed, she finally tested her strength and stood. *Wow*. Weak as a kitten.

Walking the few steps to the connected bathroom wore her out. After resting for several minutes on the vanity seat, she was able to drag her worn-out butt into the shower.

While washing her hair for the first time in days, she thought about the hours ahead. An evil idea popped into her head for the photo shoot. Guy wouldn't know what hit him.

The poor man.

# CHAPTER NINE

"**N**o way in hell am I putting that gunk on my face!"

Guy watched as Rori argued with the hair and makeup stylist. Her contract did say she could style her shoots, but he should have known that would include hair and makeup.

The session taking place in the media building was unlike any other photo shoot they had set up. Hordes of makeup people, stylists, clothes, and trunks of supplies were stacked in a high pile forming a mini-fortress. Rori would be the first female to grace the cover of SG magazine, so this was important to his staff. It was also a big deal for her, and she might be turning on the drama a bit, but he could see her point. She didn't do glam, didn't need it or want it, and was very vocal about it.

He was about to step in when he heard her offer a compromise, less makeup and more hair. After a few minutes, the hair and makeup team stepped back and revealed their efforts. The result was Rori's ethereal face with a hint of glossy, pink lips, and rocking a Mohawk ponytail.

Definitely hot.

He thought the photos would turn out amazing. She had selected a green vest, camouflage shorts, military style boots, and a huge black watch with a built-in compass from the available wardrobe. The image of her in this outfit while holding a pistol would absolutely haunt his dreams. Her image would probably haunt every man who saw the cover.

He hadn't asked her out yet. He was still working up the nerve. His usual confidence had been removed, and his nerves had gone haywire after the phone call with her father. Edward had given his permission to ask her out, but he also had seemed certain that she wouldn't mix business with pleasure.

Guy thought Edward was just being a father, but his negativity had flowed through the phone line. He just needed to shake it off.

That was all.

But watching her work as she posed for the camera, the doubt set in again. He realized how professional she really was. All business during this shoot, she was focused. She had barely glanced at him as she seemed to be in her element.

She had a vision. And from what he could see so far, her vision was dead-on. He tried to place his personal feelings aside, and the businessman in him started brainstorming.

Entering ideas in his smartphone, he missed Brock strutting in. Damn. Why did the guy keep showing up? Brock stood in front of the photo shoot and watched Rori pose. He clapped and hooted for her.

That was enough. Guy finally had it with his best friend flirting with her. "Hey, Brock, take a step back. You are crowding the session. Better yet, leave."

Brock turned and had a big grin plastered on his face. He walked toward Guy, and even though he was much shorter than Guy, he moved closer still. "Oh, really. Is this the editor talking or my best friend getting all jealous? Dude, we are not seniors, and Rori is not Melanie Milsap."

While he was staring down Brock, Brianne came marching in. Hells bells!

"Bri, what you are doing here?"

She should have been working in the middle of the day. "Please tell me that you didn't quit this job, too?" She still had on her gun shop t-shirt. Brianne's out-of-office attire always included something leather, and she was sans leather at the moment.

In typical fashion, she went from zero to sixty in thirty seconds. "No, I didn't quit my job, you jackass!" Then, calming down to about thirty, "I'm taking Rori to the day spa." Bri then looked down at her red nails innocently.

Able to read his sister better than Guy, Brock chimed in, "I don't believe you, Bri. What are you up to?"

Red hot again, she angrily replied, "Fine, if you must know, my boss put me up to it. He wants Rori to visit the shop. He heard me talking about her and he thinks that it would be good business to get her to visit. I thought I would sweeten her up a bit by taking her to the spa first."

Frustrated, Guy tossed his hands up in the air. "Between you and Brock, I'm never going to get any work done."

She shrugged and said, "Well, at least I'm offering to take her to an afternoon of relaxation after she has worked on your dumb ol' magazine cover all day!"

Brock laughed. "Who said I wasn't going to relax her?"

Guy started toward Brock, but Brianne wedged herself between them. "Boys. Calm down. How about I go ahead and invite Rori while you two cool it? Okie dokie?"

Guy apologized to Bri. She was right—he did need to calm down. Something about the way Brock looked at Rori just pissed him off to no end, and he could no longer rationalize his feelings. In this instance, Brianne was right. He needed a break.

"Fine."

Jumping up and down, she squealed with glee at the same time Rori approached. "What's all the ruckus? Did someone win the lottery?"

"Yes," said Bri, "you did! I'm taking you out for manicures and pedicures!"

Guy considered Rori's cool expression. "Are we done here, Mr. Matthews?"

He looked for confirmation from the photographer. At his nod, Guy gave his approval, "Yes, go. Bri, call me, and I will come pick Rori up later."

"No need, big brother, I can drop her off at your hotel, err…cabin."

Rori, still calm and cool, replied, "Let me tame down my hair, jot my thoughts down from this session, and I will be ready to go."

In less than fifteen minutes, Guy and Brock stood and

watched as Brianne escorted Rori to the parking lot, talking non-stop of course. "I almost feel sorry for Rori."

Brock grimaced. "Me too, man. Me too."

* * *

"Brianne, Kirsten, thank you so much for this. I needed a break." Rori sat under an umbrella at a local day spa, sipping a drink with an umbrella in it as her shoulders were massaged.

On the drive to the spa, Brianne had raved about the new massage therapist, Kirsten. Unfortunately, Kirsten was booked for the day and only had a half-hour to split between them. So, Rori was now getting a quick shoulder massage following her pedicure. This was a rare treat for her, and she really did appreciate Bri taking her to this spa.

Brianne had explained all about her boss and the gun shop, and they had stopped at the shop for the required visit before the spa. Now, they had the rest of the afternoon to relax and even shop in the old town square. Rori wanted to get her dad a souvenir from one of the western shops and hoped she could find a unique gift for him.

Brianne thanked Kirsten, and asked, "Can I book an appointment with you for my brother? He has been a pain in the neck lately and really needs to loosen up."

Kirsten was a shy, brown-haired, petite woman dressed in the spa uniform of black pants, and black, short-sleeved shirt. She had surprisingly strong hands. Softly, she said, "Of course, just stop by the receptionist desk on your way out."

Brianne turned down her shoulder massage when it was her

turn, and told Rori after they were alone, "I'm seriously going to send Brock in for a massage. Kirsten is single and new to town. Just think of all the free massages I would probably get if she started dating my brother."

Brianne was incorrigible, and Rori couldn't stop the giggle and the thought of sweet Kirsten dating the womanizing Brock. If it would ever happen.

"Plus, I'm immensely enjoying being away from my crabby boss for the afternoon."

Rori picked up an apple on the side table and bit into it. "Why do you work there if he is so grumpy?"

Bri shifted in her seat, and Rori realized that the woman was uncomfortable with that question. "I'm sorry, you don't have to answer that."

"No, I don't, but I will. I like you, Rori. I think you are genuine. I work there because it is the only job I have held down for longer than a year. I've been sort of drifting from job to job for some time. This one may stick."

So, Bri had history that chose her career similar to her own past directing her to police work. She could appreciate that. Instead of asking more questions, she let Bri add what she wanted to.

"I hope my old boss will eventually retire, and I can buy the shop." She said this so softly Rori could almost guess this was the first time she had uttered her wish aloud.

"I think that is wonderful." She really did—she didn't give false compliments to fill the gaps in conversation or to be nice. "I think if you have found your niche in life, you go for it."

Bri brightened at her words. "Yeah, I really like teaching the concealed carry classes for women, and I hope to expand into other classes in the community. One dear to my heart is teaching gun awareness in the high schools."

Rori thought that was an excellent idea. "Have you mentioned this to Guy or Brock? I'm sure they could offer you some advice."

Sitting up further in her chair, Bri nearly shouted, "No! Those two and Tucker are nothing but negative when it comes to anything I want to do. They didn't even think I could hold this job down for as long as I have. Almost every time I see Guy, he asks me if I have quit."

Yep, she had seen those three men in action when it came to Bri. It seemed that Bri had a lot to prove to herself without feeling the pressure from the men in her life. "If I were in your shoes, I probably wouldn't tell them my plans either."

Her new friend smiled smugly. "Thanks, I knew I was right."

"Can I ask you one last question?" Rori asked. At Brianne's nod, she continued. "Tell me exactly, who is Tucker?"

"Tucker Abrams is my best friend. I've known him since I was eight and he was ten."

Rori digested that piece of information. "So, twenty years of friendship? That's all he is to you?"

Bri gave a smile which made her seem far older than her twenty-eight years. "Yeah. Just friends. Off and on. Usually on, but we have been through some tough times together. Tuck is a hard man to please. Always pushing me, like Brock and Guy. No girl needs three men acting like her brothers. Can you imagine the nerve of those two today? Fighting in the middle of your soon-to-be-famous cover shoot!"

Rori allowed Bri the change of subject to Brock and Guy, but she knew that there was more to her saga with Tucker. "No, I can't believe them. Guy is always so calm. I have only seen him upset around Brock. And the cover is not going to be famous. It was in one of the SG facilities, we had lukewarm coffee, and Guy picked up bagels and donuts for breakfast on our way into town. Nothing glamorous there."

Waving her hand in front of her, Brianne protested, "Honey, you were glamorous. That cover is going to be the talk of the town, and my boss is going to have a copy of it plastered to his wall for bragging rights."

Rori knew Brianne's boss had been thrilled with her visit and had even requested a photo with her. "When the cover does come out, tell your boss that I will autograph his copy and the picture of us together at his shop."

"I will hold you to that." Brianne sat back and relaxed for a bit before asking, "What kind of dirt do you want to know about Guy?"

Rori thought this over for a bit. "Nothing."

Brianne laughed, then yelled, "Are you sure? I know all kinds of juicy stuff about my adopted brother. If I were in your place, I would want you to give me the unabridged version."

"No, really. I want to get to know him on my own, without any preconceived notions of him. You *could* tell me about the *band* he and Brock started together."

"Agreed." She continued to regale Rori with crazy stories of Brock and Guy in an air band for the next hour. Listening, Rori could picture the trouble those two caused in high school. Brock, a young Greek god, and Guy, she imagined as young Tom Selleck without the 'stache.

"I'd like to see photos of the talent contests they were in." Rori jumped in between Bri's rip-roaring tales.

The woman sure could tell a story. She had laughed so hard during the entire story and was now crying from that laughter. "Sure," she said, wiping tears from her eyes, "I'll see what I can scrounge up at mom's house."

Rori really did want to see these pictures. "I appreciate it, and I really do appreciate this afternoon." She smiled at Brianne.

Brianne's phone rang. "Sorry, it may be my crabby boss." Pulling her phone out, she looked at the number calling, "Guy," she grumbled, and then answered. "What?"

Rori could hear Guy's voice over the phone as he spoke. She couldn't make out what he was saying, but just the sound of his voice made her realize she had missed him during these last few hours. A yearning down below signaled to her that she was too far gone.

Earlier, under the heat of lamps, hair, and makeup, it had taken all her resolve to keep her cool. She had tried a cool, model attitude during the shoot, or her interpretation of a model's attitude, and hoped that she had Guy wanting her as much as she wanted him.

She continued to listen to Guy question Bri. Her friend gave short answers and then said, "I told you that I would bring her to your cabin. We still have shopping to do. Chill." With that, she ended the call with a smirk on her face. "Honey, I think you drove Guy and Brock to fight after we left. Can you believe it? He's got it bad for you."

"A fight? A real fist fight?"

"From what he just said, yes, a real fist fight. Guy picked Brock up and removed him to the parking lot. Brock, being the hot-head that he is, didn't take too kindly to that kind of treatment, so he slugged him."

Shrugging as if she wasn't surprised, Rori asked, "Is Guy all right?" A different type of woman would have jumped up and demanded to see him right away. Not her. She had hung out with dudes for so long that she was used to the roughness that went with them. She'd seen best friends tackle each other over the last onion ring, so she wasn't surprised at Brock and Guy. She had felt the tension between them during the concert and again today during her mission to torture Guy.

Bri confirmed he was fine, just sporting a bruise on his chin. She guessed he was angrier with himself than Brock. Now, if she could just get him to break first, he would be putty in her hands.

*Crap.* She couldn't believe she was sitting here planning a covert seduction of Guy Matthews. Never in a million years, or at least not in the last four, had she imagined wanting another man. But here she sat...wanting Guy Matthews to be her perfect man. She could see years of happiness before them. Working, playing, laughing, and loving each other. *Whoa, girl! Slow down here.*

Fingers snapped in front of her face. "Hello, Earth to Rori!" Bri fairly shouted into her ear. Who knew how long she had been sitting there daydreaming about white picket fences with Guy.

"Sorry."

"You and Guy just need to go at it like bunnies, and then all this tension and daydreaming will go away!"

"Bri!" She felt heat on her face. She wasn't used to being talked to that way, but found she wasn't offended and laughed at the other woman. Was this how girlfriends interacted? Bri's treatment of her made her feel included.

"What? It's true…and I will always be truthful with you. Besides, I have a feeling that we are going to be great friends." Standing, Brianne smoothed her black gun shop t-shirt and set her drink on the table. "Let's go shopping."

They enjoyed an hour or two of shopping before loading back up in Brianne's battered little SUV. It had seen better days, but it was clean, inside and out. Rori guessed that Brianne used organization as a means of control. She had seen it many times in the dorms at college, and during her brief time on the force. When life couldn't be controlled, some people cleaned or resorted to negative means to control their environments. In Rori's line of work, and away at college, she had seen some girls starve themselves. Thankfully, Bri didn't appear to be drastic. She hoped their friendship would grow, and they could lean on each other.

Ever since her mom had passed away, Rori missed deep conversations. It seemed Bri needed a friend as well. It must have been hard growing up in her brother's shadow.

Much like Rori growing up with the need to please her dad.

*Ahh, stop thinking about Edward.* The guilt was going to kill her. Her dad would be fine. He'd had four years to grieve, and he seemed to be doing well. He hadn't seemed upset on the phone when she and Guy had told him about signing the contract.

Guy was the sweetest man she had ever met. He had been so kind to her, nursing her while she was sick.

She couldn't wait to reach his cabin. She didn't know which direction their relationship was headed after today's session and his fight with Brock, but she was sitting on the edge of the car seat with anticipation.

# CHAPTER TEN

Brianne dropped Rori off later than he'd expected. Guy waited for her to notice the bruise on his jaw, but she looked straight at his face. Nothing. He figured Bri had told her about the fight and Rori didn't need to comment on it. Even if it were only to call him and Brock stupid for acting like boys instead of grown men.

Brock had certainly knocked him a good one. It had been exactly what he needed—the shit knocked out of him. Brock had even helped him to his feet, saying, "You're welcome, Matthews."

Guy had even listened when his friend offered dating advice. "Just go for it," he had told him. He wasn't certain. Not certain at all.

Rori walked past him as she took her bags to the guest room, accidentally colliding her hip with his. He felt the heat of her skin through her clothes.

"Sorry, I need to go to my room for a moment." Evidently, their brief touch didn't burn her to the core as it did him.

A few minutes later she emerged with a sundress on. "I need a second opinion, a sane one. Bri would have bought the entire store. What do you think? Should I keep it or return it before I leave for Ohio? I don't usually buy this sort of thing."

The dress was simple, bright blue, and made for her body. Clearing his throat, he walked closer to her. This was it.

He couldn't hold back anymore and leaned in to kiss her.

It was mind-blowing. Her lips were sweet and soft, and when she murmured his name, he lost it. He wrapped his arms tight around her waist. Then with one hand, he tugged her pony-tail until he gained deeper access. She snuggled closer. Their bodies didn't have an inch between them. She moved her hands from his shoulders and ran them through his hair.

He needed to touch her skin. His right hand tangled in her hair as he removed her hair clip and then moved to her throat. Moving her dress strap aside, he put his lips where his hand had been. His lips on her hot throat seemed to undo her.

"I think we need to slow down," she said as she fisted her hands in his hair. Guy understood her words, but his body didn't. His left arm still pulled her snug against him while his right hand stroked her arm.

Finally, his brain started to work again. He pulled his mouth away from her throat with a groan and said, "I know, but I'm not going to get a wink of sleep with you down the hall."

"I didn't mean stop. I meant slow down." After that unsure statement, she started to tremble. He had never seen her so shaken.

"I can do slow."

She leaned in for another kiss. "Yes."

Scooping her up, he threw her over his shoulder as she laughed loudly.

* * *

Later, he nuzzled his face against her soft skin, he breathed in her scent. "I love the way you smell."

If he could wake up next to her every day for the rest of his life, it wouldn't be enough.

Infatuated, in lust, in love. Yes, he loved her, and from the look in her eyes now, she reciprocated his love.

"What is it, sweetheart?"

"I just thought you should know…I have only done this one other time. A *long* time ago."

Guy smiled at her reassuringly, but on the inside, he melted. Such an honest confession at that moment just made him love her more. It also boosted his ego—she could be with any man she wanted, but she had chosen him.

After, he laid his head on her and she ran her fingers through his hair. He pulled himself up and lifted her into his arms. "Let's try out my huge shower before we both fall asleep."

* * *

*Heaven.* That's what waking up in Guy's arms felt like. Rori stretched a bit and felt a few muscles protest. Other than those muscles, lack of sleep, and a heavy arm cutting off her air, this was, indeed, heaven.

Sensations kept rolling over her as she thought back to last night. What a night. she couldn't think about that shower without getting hot and bothered again.

Twisting a bit, she eased out from beneath his arm. Tiptoeing to the bathroom, she did her business, brushed her teeth, combed her hair, and rushed back to the bed.

He was awake and waiting for her. "Morning."

"Good morning to you, Mr. Matthews." Climbing back into bed, she barely touched her head to the pillow before he pulled her to his side of the bed with one arm.

She could get used to this.

Snuggling in with him under the covers, she said the first thing that popped into her head. "Was it good for you?"

He roared with laughter. "I think that is my line."

She hit him hard on the arm. "Seriously, Matthews!"

"I know, and that is why you are just so darn adorable, beautiful, sexy…" Each complimentary word was followed by a kiss. He kissed her forehead, chin, and temple. All areas which normally wouldn't get her heart racing, but any kiss given by Guy seemed to have that race-car effect on her. She had to be serious before he got completely out of hand this morning.

Pulling away from him for a second, she said, "Guy. Be serious. I want to know." She waited for what seemed forever.

"Rori, last night was amazing. We were amazing together. Tell me what is going on in that head of yours." He pushed back the hair that had fallen into her eyes. Staring at him and seeing his concern, she knew that she had to bring up the past. Airing out the dirty laundry after last night seemed like closing the barn door after the horse had bolted, but she had to get the episode from college off her chest.

Blowing out an unladylike sigh, she started. "Remember last night how I said that I had only done this one other time?"

He nodded encouragingly while rubbing her arm. She began again, telling her college experience for the first time to anyone. She hadn't even told her mother. She'd been too embarrassed.

"Well, my freshman year of college, I was a naïve eighteen-year-old. I was so glad to live my own life. For the first time, I was undisciplined, and I let my guard down." She looked up, expecting him to interject something, but he just continued to rub her arm soothingly. "I met Quintin the first week of college. Yes, he came from money, as you could tell with that ridiculous name, but that had nothing to do with my attraction to him. Quintin was handsome and fun. He didn't know that Aurora Cross from New Brick, Ohio was a complete tomboy. You see, before college, my mother and I went shopping. And...for the first time in my life, I shopped for style, not function."

At Guy's raised eyebrows, she stopped to explain, "Highlights, new clothes, makeup, I wanted to be a completely new me. My wardrobe hadn't been selected based on durability."

She paused as she thought back to what she was saying. "As the new Aurora, I started dating Quintin. I had never even been kissed before, and he thought it was sweet that I was so innocent. We spent almost every day together for two months. We played Frisbee in the park, ran, hiked, and of course studied together."

He did say something then. "It sounds like the two of you had much in common."

"We did, but it was all a lie. At least for Quintin it was a lie. He had another girlfriend back home. You know, one of those rich girls. His parents probably picked her out for him. All I was to him was a naïve girl from some small, hick town he had never heard of."

Guy kissed her forehead. "How did you discover the truth about Quintin?"

"We were at a party, not too long after he and I had, well, you know…and I overheard him talking to his rich buddies about me. Evidently, I had been a bet, just a dumb bet. I meant nothing to him. The party was a fraternity party. They were all standing in a circle, in their cute little polo shirts. I watched Quintin stick out his hand to one of his buddies. 'You owe me fifty dollars,' and my heart broke into a million pieces."

"What did you do to him?"

Propped up on one elbow, she asked, "What makes you think I did something to him?"

Those dark eyes stared down at her with a look that said, *I know you.* "Fine, I walked right over to him and his buddies. They stopped drinking from their plastic cups. It was so quiet. I didn't say anything. I just took my knee and I dropped that asshole to the ground. I walked out, and never looked back."

Lost in the past for a minute, she didn't speak. Guy hugged her to him again and said, "The asshole is just lucky you didn't shoot him."

. . .

Leave it to him to try to clear the air with humor. But she had one more thing to say related to Quintin. "I know it seems drastic, but I haven't trusted another man since, until you."

"I feel the same way about you, sweetheart."

Now it was her turn to tease. "You haven't trusted men either?" Grinning widely, she pressed her lips against his and wrestled him onto his back. She must have had an evil look because he started to look worried. "Rori, what are you doing?"

"Tickle torture!"

He let her have her way for a few moments. Finally, she let up so he could breathe.

After catching his breath, he said, "I have an important question for you. Have you ever been floating?"

"Floating? What the heck is that?"

# CHAPTER ELEVEN

T he romantic, scenic floating trip had been exactly as he'd planned. No ripples, water or emotional. Rori had enjoyed it, and Guy had enjoyed showing her his favorite part of Wyoming—Moose, both the town and the animal.

Floating on the Snake River had been one of the few outdoorsy things he and his parents had done together as a family. His doctor parents weren't active people, although they both belonged to gyms, they didn't exert themselves outside. No grass cutting, no gardening, and no pets.

His mother did have a love of sunsets, though. So, his father made the occasional attempt at romance, and floating had eventually become a family activity.

Guy had done this trip so many times that he didn't need a guide, but since this was Grand Teton National Park, one had to be authorized to conduct a float tour. So, he had rented the entire evening, since he didn't want to woo his lady with others gawking at them. The tour guide he had to put up with, though.

Rori sighed and drew his attention to her. She was staring up at the moon while lying flat on her back in the campsite at their take-out spot. She had received a few messages on her cell phone earlier, and he assumed they were from her father. He was glad they were finally in an area where cell service was impossible. A fire before them, they had just eaten the cold sandwiches and salads he had brought for them. Sure, they could fish and really rough it, but she had done so much of that growing up, he just wanted her to enjoy their evening without fish guts all over her new blouse. Beneath that calm, cool attitude was a warm, feminine woman. And this woman was proving to be a true romantic at heart. Her love of old movies complemented an affinity for sundresses, the color pink, lacy blouses, and pedicures. Add the rock-n-roll, a deadly aim, and a heavenly figure, and she was a tough nut to crack.

He didn't know whether to hug her or challenge her to a race. So far, he had gone for the hugs. He assumed that Sallie Cross had been the only person to be affectionate with her. She was starved of human contact, which was probably why that jerk Quintin was able to get close to her.

Edward Cross had so effectively transformed his daughter into a tomboy that she was all over the map. Not that Guy minded, but he wanted to be right there while she found herself again.

Hopefully, she wouldn't mind camping tonight in her pink blouse, shorts, and trail sandals. She had appreciated floating down the river. Armed with a water-proof camera she had borrowed from the magazine, she had snapped picture after picture of trees, birds, and other wildlife. She had been a sponge all afternoon, soaking up the information that their old guide, Tom, had provided to her. Tom, or Handlebar Tom as he was known on the Snake River, had helped them make camp, and then promised to be back in the morning to drive them back to town.

Guy planned on camping right beside the peaceful water in a little blue tent he had used for years, with only the fire for warmth and the possibility of sharing some body heat.

It didn't seem possible that he had found the only woman for him just a few short days ago. Here they were sitting beside one another in comfortable silence enjoying the moon. He didn't have to ask her what she was thinking. He knew.

She wanted to stay here…with him.

And he wanted her here with him. He couldn't stand the thought of her going back to Ohio. He could always go with her. Assist her with moving, telling Edward, resigning from the police force, kicking Dwayne in the teeth. The latter he would very much enjoy.

What exactly would they be telling her boss and her father? That yes, she was now a full-time SG spokesperson and writer for the magazine? Or, that, yes, they had fallen in love and couldn't be apart more than a few hours, let alone days?

Those three little words had yet to be spoken. He felt them, but a part of him was terrified that those words would scare her. As much as she had opened up to him this morning, she was still very closed off.

The past couple days, even when she had been sick, he had

seen her laugh more and connect with more people. She had been civil the few times he had seen her interact with her co-workers, but her behavior toward them wouldn't be called friendly.

It seemed being away from the worry of New Brick, and her responsibilities, had her eyes full of hope now.

Standing, Guy rolled his cargos down and was about to go get more kindling to put on the fire. He caught her eyes and he imagined her asking *need help*? Wordlessly, he reached out a hand and pulled her to her feet. They worked together gathering the kindling. Compatible in almost every way, he still couldn't believe how lucky he was to have found her, a teammate in all areas of his life.

Walking back to the campsite, she said, "You haven't mentioned the photo shoot at all. Have I just completely side-tracked you?"

Dropping his load of kindling, he took her load from her as he crouched, adding small branches to the fire. "I have been sidetracked, but that isn't why I haven't said anything. I didn't mention it because I wanted last night and today to be about us, not about the magazine."

Her blue eyes widened upon hearing his words. "I think that is one of the nicest things anyone has ever said to me."

"How about…I love you?"

She coughed, and he didn't know what to think.

"Rori, did you hear me?"

"You love me?"

"Yes, I love you." Finding it tough to swallow, he waited… and waited some more.

"Good," she said as she punched his arm. He could tell she wanted to say the words, but she dodged the issue. He understood. Let her feel secure again in all areas of her life before demanding the same declaration from her.

Finally grabbing hold of her arm, he pulled her to him and enveloped her. "Now, about that photo shoot."

They spent the next hour in front of the fire writing down ideas for Rori's SG career. Guy felt that she should brand herself as a calm, cool, butt-kicking, hot chick. He flipped out his phone and rattled off about ten different ideas.

"When did you come up with all this?" she asked, startled.

"During the shoot, before Brock showed up."

Some of his ideas rocked. One, a live, weekly web show with the ability to reach tons of viewers.

Her only contribution to his ten ideas was her blog. A stupid little blog. He encouraged her, though, by telling her a blog, along with other social media, was needed and he would help her re-vamp all of it.

Her dad would be able to do all this for her, but she didn't want him to, and wasn't about to ask him. That was how different her life had become in a week. She wanted Guy and the magazine staff to train her, mentor her. The old Rori would've let her daddy do it for her. But this would allow her the opportunity to learn a new skill and develop more self-confidence. Her other idea for the blog was to interview women, or have guest bloggers, all women. Her first choice would be Bri.

Guy hadn't laughed at her choice, and a plan for tomorrow and a new SG blog called, *Rocking with Rori*, or something similar, was in the works.

For the first time in over four years, she was excited to go to work in the morning. This was actually going to be her full-time job. She couldn't wait to get back to New Brick and start packing.

Guy loved her, and she loved him, but she wasn't about to tell him. Show him, maybe, but the telling could wait because every time she thought she would say the words, she felt tears form. Tears! Aurora Cross did not cry. Until she could get a handle on her emotions and not cry like a blubbering ninny, she would just show Guy how much she loved him.

They sat and chatted for over an hour until she decided it was time to go to bed. "Matthews, let's go to sleep." She was still going for the detached attitude.

He rose and threw some water on the fire. "I don't think we need this tonight." Together they walked to the little blue tent, and he unzipped it and pulled back one side for her to enter.

She felt confident and reminded herself that he wasn't Quintin. He wasn't a liar or a manipulator. Looking at him, she felt her heart swell with love.

She had to get a grip on her emotions, they were so powerful. She had never felt this way about Quintin. That must have been puppy love. Or lust. Whatever it was, it wasn't this swelling, heart-tugging, tear-jerking feeling that consumed her.

"Rori, sweetheart. Where are you?" She looked at Guy again. How could her mind get so distracted while she was with this gorgeous man?

"I'm right here." Closing the book on her past, she opened a new one for the present. She leaned down and kissed him as she wanted to kiss him. All of this culminated with falling asleep, legs tangled, on top of a sleeping bag in a small, blue tent beside a river in Wyoming.

Amazing.

The last thing she remembered before she was dead to the world was Guy kissing her temple and whispering that he loved her. For the second night in a row, she fell asleep with a grin on her face.

* * *

"Guy, aren't you going to introduce us?"

They were enjoying a meal at the local IHOP after their float guide, Handlebar Tom, had dropped them off at Guy's Tahoe. Instead of heading straight home, they had decided to stay in town for breakfast and stroll around a bit after.

They had just been served their food when a sultry voice interrupted. Rori watched the Marilyn Monroe wanna-be sway over to their table, easing her way next to Guy on his side of the booth.

Guy's jaw clenched, and his hand tightened around his fork. She hoped he didn't plan on using it as a weapon. Whoever this lady was, he didn't like her.

The ghost of Marilyn had on a white sundress, high heels, and bright red lips. Rori almost introduced herself, but Guy finally grumbled, "Bambi, meet Rori."

Digging back into his eggs, he pretended Bambi wasn't an

inch from him and trying to suck up his air. Who the heck was this chick?

Bambi extended a perfectly manicured hand. In a sweet voice, she said, "Bambi Matthews. Pleased to meet you. Any friend of Guy's is a friend of mine."

*Crap.* Rori had a sense that something was not right. Hoping that her gut instinct was wrong, she asked, "Are you related to Guy?"

They answered at the same time. His venomous, "No" almost overrode Bambi's gleeful, "Yes."

Rori sank back in her seat and took a sip of orange juice. Guy rubbed his hands over his face. She had a terrible feeling this was gonna get ugly.

Bambi laughed and patted Guy on the arm. "Oh, sugar, I'm his wife."

Rori choked on her juice. He reached over to assist her while saying, "Ex-wife…for five years now."

Numbly, Rori repeated, "Ex-wife for five years?"

Stupid Bambi laughed again. "Sugar, he couldn't wait to get those divorce papers signed after he found out about Benny and me. Luckily, he still sends my alimony check every month, so I don't have too much to complain about."

*What a nightmare!* She kept repeating back everything that Guy and Bambi had said. "Benny?"

Guy grumbly answered her question. "Benny is Bambi's ski instructor boyfriend. They won't get married so they can continue to live off my money."

Rori was in shock. She knew the signs. She was a police officer, for crying out loud. It was hard to admit, but her feelings were hurt. He had been married to someone else and had never told her. She thought she was important, that she mattered to him. What a fool she had been…pouring out her heart and telling the embarrassing tale of her college mistake with Quintin.

Guy jumped in. "Bambi, please leave. You got what you came for, which was to stir the pot."

"Fine, sugar. By the way, good luck on your magazine award. I hear from Brock that you have it in your sights with this cute little doll working for you now." Bambi took his coffee cup, drank from it, and slid out of the booth. To give Guy credit, he pushed the cup away with disgust.

"Wow," Rori whispered, still processing what had just happened. Guy had an awful ex-wife and had been using her to win an award. *Just wow…*

"Is that true? Are you using me for a magazine award?"

"No, sweetheart. It's true that I coveted that award for years. I thought of it when I went out to meet you and mentioned it to Brock. But, after meeting you, and knowing you, I haven't given the award another thought."

She believed him. What did that say about her? Needing some time to think, she pulled out her cell phone and noticed a missed text from her father.

*Confirmed-Dwayne knows where you are. May be headed that way.*

She needed to get the heck out of Dodge. Dwayne may try to shoot Guy again. Her head started to hurt thinking about that scenario, and right now her chest ached over this Bambi busi-ness. She was certain she would eventually get over it. She had a past as well, but one thing she couldn't get over was Dwayne hurting someone she loved. She took a deep breath and proceeded to leave Guy in order to save him.

*Forgive me, Guy.*

He reached for her hand. "Rori, do you believe me?"

"No," she lied. "Give me the keys."

"Rori, I should have told you before, but—"

Now, she had gone from shock to just plain scared and pissed off. "Give me your freaking keys to the Tahoe."

Sitting up on one hip to dig into his pocket, he pulled out his keys and slid them across the table. "Go calm down. We can talk when you are ready."

She tried a different tactic to ensure he didn't follow her. "Don't tell me to calm down, and don't come back to your lodge until I am gone. I will have Brianne take me to the airport. I'm warning you, Guy, don't follow me, and don't call me unless it is about SG business."

She said everything quietly while leaning in toward Guy to avoid alerting other diners that they were arguing. Getting out of the booth, she grabbed his keys and walked out the door.

Late that night, Guy opened his front door to Brock.

"You know? Let me guess, Bri?"

Brock patted him on the shoulder and walked in without being asked. "Little sister called all pissed off. Bambi was the worst mistake you ever made, but that doesn't explain why you didn't tell Rori about being married before and that stupid award."

"I was a fool. Bambi took me for a fool. What man wants to admit that? And when did you run into Bambi, telling her about my business?"

Brock tucked his head down in apology. "Sorry, man, she came up beside me at the Crooked Lane, I'd had one too many beers. Her dress was low, and…"

"Enough. I get the picture. She manipulated you—as always."

"Thanks, man, but why didn't you follow Rori? Why did you let her leave? She is the best thing that has ever happened to you. And you wuss out and just let her leave. No fight?"

"Let it be, Brock. I don't see you fighting for the woman you love."

"I haven't found her. That's why. If I had someone like Rori, don't you think I wouldn't fight for her with everything I've got?"

"Thanks, but no thanks, Brock. I'm not having a heart-to-heart with you about Rori."

"Man, don't let a stupid mistake from over five years ago ruin your relationship with Rori. At least explain it to her."

"She wants nothing to do with me."

Brock punched him in the shoulder, a little too hard to be friendly, but his words registered. "Now you are just being plain stupid. Get your ass in gear and get on the next plane to Ohio."

Then Brock left. Brianne must have really ripped him one for his friend to come all the way out here to tell him he was stupid.

And he was. He had married Bambi six years ago because he wanted to get married, and ticking off his parents by choosing someone they disliked was a bonus. Not something he was proud of, but he was human. And weak. Bambi was attractive, funny, or so he had thought. He hadn't wanted to be stuck with Bambi in a loveless marriage, but he had wanted to be married, work hard, win awards, and raise children. He thought that maybe one day he would love her. He liked her, and she claimed to love him. So, they had married quickly, and he had started building the lodge. Eight weeks later, he had found her in bed with Benny. She had demanded a divorce, seeing dollar signs in the divorce settlement and alimony payments. She had quit her job as a waitress and continued to live off her alimony payments.

Guy hadn't fought too much after finding out about Benny, he had just wanted it over with. And he preferred not to have the entire town know what a fool he had been. But they had ended up knowing that anyway.

Benny and Bambi were very affectionate and lived in town. All on his dime.

He didn't run into her often, but when he did, she pestered the shit out of him. Today, of all days, why hadn't he just taken Rori back to the lodge? Never in a million years had he thought that they would run into Bambi.

Sure, it looked bad. From Rori's side of the fence it looked even worse. *Damn it.* His one big mistake may have ruined his chances with her. He wanted her, loved her. He thought she loved him too. But the ticked-off look in her eyes—and maybe a little hurt—when she had demanded his keys this morning…that look would haunt him.

He had to see her and explain to her why he hadn't told her about his marriage and divorce. Dialing the airlines and booking the earliest flight to Ohio, Guy had a scary thought—he hoped she wasn't holding a gun when he tracked her down.

# CHAPTER TWELVE

"**D**ad!"

Rori rushed up the stairs to her father's house. It was early, but her father was an early bird. She had been surprised when she hadn't found him at the kitchen table, fully dressed for his workday, drinking his coffee, eating a piece of peanut butter toast, and planning ways to catch Dwayne.

Her father was a very methodical, structured person. She could drive each night of the week and find her father at his standard dinner at various restaurants. His breakfast routine, though, never varied—coffee, grapefruit, and then peanut butter on toast.

When her mom had been alive, Edward had a full breakfast prepared for him every morning. The bacon he used to consume hadn't helped his heart, but every time Sallie Cross had substituted his bacon with turkey bacon, the man had thrown a fit.

Poor Edward. Rori was sure that her dad had some regrets. Her mother had just tried to keep him healthy.

Reaching the landing, she called out again. "Dad? Are you here?"

She heard some grumbling from her father's bedroom door, and then she thought she heard another voice. "Dad, did you fall asleep with the TV on?" she asked as she pushed open his bedroom door.

On one side of the room stood her father in obvious shock. And on the other was Miss Stanwick, the New Brick librarian.

Understanding the scene before her, she said, "I didn't know the librarian would come and collect your overdue books, Dad." And with that rude comment, she spun on her heels and almost flew down the stairs.

She didn't know if her father called after her. She ran to her truck and pulled out of the gravel drive. Her tires spun out a bit in her haste to get the hell away from what she just saw.

It wasn't until she had made it back to her condo and could barely see to pull into her lot that she realized that she was crying. This couldn't be happening. Her dad loved her mom so much that there was no way he had moved on.

No way!

That Miss Stanwick had seduced her dad. That's what had happened. She had seen his vulnerability and swooped in like a four-eyed vulture. Her father was a respectable man and would never have a secret affair. Never.

*Calm down, Rori.*

The best way to calm down was at the range. Running into

her condo and then into her gun room, she grabbed what she needed, locked up, and headed back to her truck.

The range was sometimes the best place to clear her head. Many of her evenings and weekends after moving back to New Brick from college had been spent here.

She made it halfway through the box of .38 caliber bullets and was still pissed. Any bystander or local would know she was in a mood. Luckily, there weren't any bystanders in the New Brick range. It was early on a weekday morning, and most range folks were at work.

She loaded five more bullets in the cylinder and closed it until she felt it click into place. The last time she had pulled out her old Smith & Wesson revolver had been when she had been paired up with Dwayne Tealy for that brief period. The Smith & Wesson was the first gun she had ever received from her father.

The weapon was easy to use and fired true. She just plain liked the sound and feel of it. She had been shooting this gun for so long that it was her way to let off some steam.

Some girls ate chocolate when pissed off. Rori shot a .38.

She pulled back the hammer, aimed, and pulled the trigger. Used to the small kickback, she shot four more times, lowered the revolver, flipped the cylinder open, and reloaded.

The two people she trusted and loved the most in her life had betrayed her. First, there was Guy's omission about his ex-wife, and the coveted award; and second, her father and his affair. Running home and expecting comfort from her father had seemed the right idea. But she hadn't been expecting to find her father and his secret girlfriend, the local librarian.

Two weeks ago, her life hadn't been perfect. For a few days, it seemed that she had found her Mr. Perfect and a new career. Now, her father was a horny old ass, and crazy Dwayne was out there somewhere, hiding, waiting to shoot at them again.

Yep. Her life currently sucked.

Rori reached for the box of bullets she had with her and realized she had almost finished them off.

* * *

Guy and Edward watched Rori through the bulletproof glass. Both men were debating intruding on her session.

"Boy, if I were you, I would wait to talk to her. She is mighty upset about something, and she is upset with me. That is not a good combination."

Guy thought about that for a second. "I'm going to wait until she finishes that box of bullets. Then I'm going in there and talk to her. I shouldn't have let her go in the first place."

Edward scratched his head, then asked. "What did you do to set her off to begin with?"

He dropped his head and answered truthfully. "I left out the part about my ex-wife. What did you do?"

Edward lowered his voice. "I have a girlfriend."

He sputtered and coughed. That hadn't been what he had been expecting. "Well, it seems we both owe Rori some groveling."

"You're right about that, my boy. Definitely right about that." Edward continued to watch her a few more minutes before he turned to Guy and held out his hand.

He shook it. "You aren't leaving, are you?"

Edward nodded. "Yes, I am. I will get with my daughter later. I have a feeling the conversation I need to have with her is going to take longer than either of us are comfortable with. That conversation will take place in private, not here for anyone to be part of."

He left after patting Guy on the back. He genuinely liked the old grouch now. Edward cared for his daughter's feelings. There was a price to pay for his secret girlfriend, but Guy understood why he hadn't told her. No one wanted to let her down.

Guy included.

Sure, he could tell himself now that he hadn't told her about Bambi because his ex was his past. The past didn't matter, and all the other excuses he could come up with.

He now grasped that the time to have told her about his ex-wife was when she had poured her soul out to him about her college boyfriend.

Rori had given of herself while he had taken.

Man. He had screwed up.

Well, now was the time to make it right. Taking a long, deep breath, he opened the bulletproof door to the indoor shooting range. He had waited until she put her Smith & Wesson down.

Closing the door softly, he watched her turn around.

If looks could kill, he would be a dead man. The combination of his omission and what her father had done had tipped her over the edge. Brass littered the floor. Dark circles shadowed her eyes and her always perfect ponytail was a mess.

She removed her hearing protection and ignored him as she gathered up her things.

Silent treatment.

"Rori, sweetheart."

He stopped at *sweetheart* when she glared at him over her shoulder. New approach. "I'm an ass. A stupid idiot. I should have told you about Bambi…and the magazine award."

More silence.

"Please talk to me. I shouldn't have let you leave Wyoming without talking first. You were so pissed off, and I didn't want to make it worse. Instead, letting you leave has made it worse."

No reaction. Another tactic was in order. "Rori, do you think I was proud to have to been married to Bambi? Heck no. It was stupid. I was dating her and wanted to be married and start a family. The marriage was over before it began. It was so long ago. Please don't make me get on my knees and beg. I will if that is what it will take for you to turn around."

Ready to crouch down and plead some more, he didn't care that he was behaving like a groveling idiot. He had messed up and begging on his knees was his next option. He hoped it worked.

She turned and stared at him, but still didn't say anything. Her body language said *I'm listening*, so he continued with his apology. "I'm sorry. I took from you and never gave back. I should have told you about my failed marriage when you opened up to me. I'm an idiot, but I'm an idiot who loves you."

Calmly, she replied, "It is too much right now, but I am a professional, and we have to work together. I will hold my end of the contract. Don't worry about that. Please move away from the door, Mr. Matthews. I'd like to leave now."

Taking a step toward her, he pleaded once more. "Rori, please…"

Pushing his chest with her palm, she put some distance between them. "Don't say another word. You lied to me! My father lied to me, and I'm on the edge right now. Dwayne is… never mind. Please move out of my way."

Stepping to the side of the door, he had to admit that she did look angry enough to slap him, and maybe he should be worried for his safety.

Time.

That's all she needed. He would just give her time. They had a working relationship. He would just stay right here in New Brick and wait until she calmed down before discussing their relationship again. He could work remotely from his hotel room.

He loved Rori and he would wait. He knew deep down that she loved him as well. Otherwise, she wouldn't have been with him and she certainly wouldn't have opened to him about her past.

She couldn't stay mad at him forever. At least he hoped she couldn't.

\* \* \*

She could pretend to stay mad at Guy Matthews forever. He could grovel all he wanted, she wasn't about to give in anytime soon. At least not until Dwayne had either turned himself in or was arrested. Oh, no, Rori Cross could hold a grudge for a very long time, so this behavior wouldn't be abnormal for her. Hard, but not out of character. She could play this part until Dwayne was locked up.

Walking past him to exit the indoor range, she placed her

black range bag on the table while she rooted around her shorts pocket for the keys to her truck. She felt Guy right on her heels.

She turned and blasted at him. "What?"

"Rori, I know you are very pissed right now, but as you said yourself, we have spreads to work on. We need to go over the proofs from the photo shoot, and I need your final draft for your first article."

They did have work to do. "Fine, set up a time and text me."

So involved in trying not to look at Guy, she didn't notice the expensive black sedan idling in the rain directly outside the front door of the facility. A driver holding a rather large umbrella opened the back door, and a dark figure emerged. The range door opened, and the driver dropped the umbrella to expose his passenger's face. She already knew the unexpected visitor.

Jeanette Tealy was dressed as Cruella Deville in a long raincoat, her lips as red as a cherry, and her salt and pepper hair perfectly pushed back from her face.

Just what Rori needed—more drama.

"Aurora," she said shrilly. "I didn't think you would come back to this town after the hell you have put my son through."

*Great! Just freakin' great. Stay calm.* Holding her hands up in her defense, she replied, "The hell I've put your son through? Your son is a cop, and he has sworn to protect and serve. Instead, he faked his own disappearance and shot at Mr. Matthews."

Jeanette pretended she didn't hear those words and continued in her shrill voice. "You have been carrying on with my son in secret, then this one shows up, and you parade around town like a harlot. Shame on you, Aurora, and your deceitful ways. My poor son loves you, and how do you repay his love? You cheat on him."

"Whoa, lady, back up a minute. I have never had a personal relationship with Dwayne. He repulses me. He has stalked me, put a GPS device on my truck, and lord only knows what else. Your saint of a son is crazy. I think you know this, but just don't want to admit it!"

Mrs. Tealy still refused to listen to the truth. "Your job is gone, Miss Cross. Your reputation, everything you hold dear. Gone. My husband and I are going to ruin you for this."

"Hold on." Guy jumped in. "You will do nothing of the kind. Rori also works for me, and no one will be taking away her job. Also, your threats about ruining her reputation are empty. I have access to one of the biggest magazines in the U.S. It would ruin your reputation and your husband's if a story were to come out about a power-hungry family in small-town Ohio."

That statement hit Jeanette like a ton of bricks. "You wouldn't dare. We would sue your magazine so fast it would make your head spin."

"How can you sue when I have been recording this entire conversation?" Extracting his reporter's voice recorder from his pocket, Guy played back the last few minutes of their conversation."

"This isn't the end of this, Mr. Matthews." Jeanette turned and opened the door to the range. Rori and Guy watched as her driver opened her umbrella and assisted her inside the car.

"What a witch," they said in unison.

Smiling at him, Rori said, "That was a sneaky move back there. I didn't know you carried around a recorder with you."

He shrugged nonchalantly. "Something I've done since college. I carry it around to take notes for myself."

It was hard to look him in the eye and tell him thanks when she was pretending to be mad at him, so she toed the concrete floor as she said, "Well, it came in handy today. Thanks."

"I talked to your father earlier, but he didn't mention anything about Dwayne. What is the latest on his whereabouts?"

"We don't know. After Dad found the tracking device on my truck, they searched his apartment again. Nothing. Dad thinks he has a secret hideaway."

"How many properties does Dwayne's father own? I think his mother knows where he may be. Have the NB police checked all these addresses?"

"Oh, no, Guy, you stay out of this. And why do you think she knows Dwayne's whereabouts?"

"She said her son 'loves' you. Not 'loved' you. Dwayne's mother used the present tense when referring to her son. I think she has talked to him recently."

"That is a good idea, Guy, but still, stay out of the search for Dwayne. Don't go near this situation. I will mention it when I go in to work tomorrow."

"Surely you aren't starting back tomorrow? Rori, give yourself some time." He placed his hand on her arm.

She shrugged him off, gathered her bag, and exited the range with him right on her heels. She opened the driver's side door to her truck. "Just because I am grateful and now speaking to you, doesn't mean things are back to normal. Whatever that is."

He stepped back. "Fine. That's fine. Are you free tonight to go over these proofs?"

"No. I have other things to do. Make it tomorrow after work. I'll call you."

She jumped in her truck, roared the engine as much as you could make a Toyota roar, and left him standing in the rain.

Even though tonight would be better to go over the photo shoot proofs, she didn't want to agree with him. What she needed was to hightail it home and sulk.

Maybe even call Brianne?

The two of them had bonded during their spa outing, and then Bri had helped her flee Wyoming two days ago.

Nothing like getting a pedicure, taking a trip to a gun shop, and running from a relationship to bring two girls together.

She still didn't understand Brianne's brash, bite-me attitude, but she liked the woman more than any female acquaintance she had ever been around. Even though distance separated them, she hoped they would become close friends. Besides, she would be in Wyoming on several trips throughout the year to fulfill her SG obligations.

She had fallen in love with more than Guy Matthews during the past week. Her love of Wyoming was evident in the many pictures she had taken while hiking and floating on the river.

Maybe she should look into eventually getting a vacation home in Jackson Hole. A vacation place of her own, something she picked out. No influence from her father, no log cabin built by Guy for his busty ex-wife Bambi.

Nope, this place would have Rori's stamp all over it. It would be hers. Maybe it should be more than a vacation home.

Something more year-round, maybe the vacation home should be this condo. It was bought and paid for by her father.

Humph. That decision was easy!

She was leaving. Yep. She would give notice to the NBPD, but then she was done. Cross family history be damned. The added stress of the Tealys' and Dwayne's craziness had pushed her over the edge.

Smiling for the first time in days, she realized that she liked the idea of a clean slate. New job, new place, new environment. The only bad part was the current state of her relationship with Guy.

She could handle him. What she couldn't handle was staying in this town, with her lying father telling her every move to make. Her entire life, she had lived according to her father's plan for her.

No longer.

He could now manage the career path of his librarian girl-friend. Geez, she still couldn't believe her father had lied to her. Just how long had he been with Miss Stanwick? For a brief second, she thought maybe this had been going on before her mom had passed away, but she knew that was just her anger seeping through.

One truth she knew—her parents' marriage had been based on true love. Edward had loved Sallie more than his own life. Rori thought at the time her mother died that if her dad didn't die from the heart attack, he would die of a broken heart.

No, this fling with Stanwick was recent. And to give her dad credit, his new girlfriend was the New Brick catch for his age group. Miss Stanwick was attractive, employed, and had all her teeth.

She knew she was being harsh, but crap, she was mad.

Arriving at her condo parking lot, Rori put her truck in park and jumped out. Tossing her range bag over her shoulder, she almost made it to her door when she heard her name being called out.

"Rori? Can we talk?"

Miss Stanwick. *Darn it.* She turned and squared her shoulders, ready for battle. "No, I'm not really in the mood for talking."

"Rori, please," Miss Stanwick pleaded.

Whatever else could go wrong this evening, she might as well be comfortable in her own home instead of standing on her stoop. "Fine, come in."

Miss Stanwick stood nervously inside the condo. Even though she didn't want to, Rori offered her something to drink.

"Thanks, but I don't want to take up too much of your time."

"Then out with it. Did my dad send you here?" While waiting for an answer, she dropped her range bag on the table, turned, and gave the older woman what she hoped was a severe look.

"No, of course not. Eddie would not be pleased with me if he knew."

*Eddie?* Never had she heard her dad referred to as Eddie. Geez. "Why don't you have a seat and tell me why you're here."

This was taking forever. She was ready to relax and had no time for this kind of drama. Just when she was about to blow her top off, Miss Stanwick began to speak.

"Your father and I went on a secret, first date six months ago. He didn't want to hurt you. I told him I understood. As things progressed, I waited for him to come out in the open with our relationship. The thing is, Rori, he blames himself. He blames himself for your mother, for your heartbreak, moving back here and quitting college. He doesn't want to hurt you by moving on. At first, he didn't believe that he could love again, or that he deserved to be happy."

"I take it he has changed his mind?"

"Yes, he has. Seeing you with Guy changed his mind. He loves you so much, Rori, he didn't want to be in a relationship while you felt the need to take care of him and treat him like a child."

"My dad needed me."

"I don't disagree with you there, but I think you are missing part of the equation."

"What?"

"You two needed each other."

"So, now you're a therapist?"

"No, but as a librarian, I hear many stories during the day. I'm a good listener. You and Edward needed each other. Sure, you may have sacrificed college, but your father has sacrificed his entire life for you. He would die for you. Shouldn't he be happy?"

"And he would be happy with you?"

"Yes, I love him. We are good together. We are different from each other, but we complement one another."

"So, are you going to move in with him?"

"No, we are going to get married. He proposed two days

ago, and I accepted. Now though, I'm afraid that with your current situation with Guy and Dwayne, Eddie will cancel our engagement."

*Wow.*

The hits just kept coming. Her dad married to someone else?

A quick look down confirmed what Rori didn't want to believe. Sure enough, Miss Stanwick had a gleaming diamond-and-gold ring on the correct finger. She couldn't handle this right now.

"If you are done with the guilt trip, I think it is time you leave."

She held the door open wide and was surprised when Miss Stanwick stopped, looked her straight in the eye, and said, "You know I'm right. Think about your father's happiness."

She would be lying if she said she wasn't impressed that the lady didn't seem to be afraid of her, but as mad as she was, she held on to her anger and didn't slam the door as she wanted.

Had she missed the mark? Did her father just pretend to need her?

No, he truly grieved for Sallie. But a niggling thought crept into her head. Her dad had been the one to establish their every-other-night dinner and shooting practice.

She thought it had been because he was lonely. Also, he wanted to help her improve her shooting skills. What if it had been because he hadn't wanted *her* to be alone? What if all this time her dad thought he was taking care of her?

Forehead against the front door, Rori slid the chain, then walked into her master bathroom to draw her bath water. She kicked off her boots, poured a glass of wine, shrugged out of her clothes and into pajamas, and checked her messages.

One garbled message from Guy, a telemarketer, and a call from her father to call him tomorrow.

Something about the garbled message from Guy boggled her brain, but she put that down to her nerves being shot to hell today. She was *not* calling him back tonight and decided to let him stew until tomorrow.

Book, bath, a glass of wine, and then it was bed for this girl. Guy, her father, Dwayne, resigning from her job, all the drama in her life…well, it would just have to wait until tomorrow.

# CHAPTER THIRTEEN

I t seemed that Guy was going to be that guy. The guy waiting on a woman to give him the time of day.

Twice now, she had left him standing in a parking lot eating her dust. It was time to buck up. She had every right to be angry, but he still had things he wanted to say to her, and damn it, he was going to say them.

Tonight!

Pulling out his phone, he pulled up her numbers and accidentally called her house phone.

"Rori, listen…"

Guy never got to finish because a cloth was shoved over his mouth before he could get anything else out.

He tried to fight off his assailant, but a strange odor was on the cloth, and he had no other course but to breathe it in. His last thoughts before everything went dark were of Rori, and that he'd never get to tell her loved her again.

\* \* \*

This was it. Time to get his true love back.

Dwayne used his best knot-tying skills to bind the man responsible for all his recent trouble. Guy Matthews didn't look so tough tied to a chair in Dwayne's underground lair.

The lair was just a basement apartment in one of his father's warehouses, but Rori would be surprised at the length he had gone to in order to ensure she was cared for.

Two years he had worked on this hideaway, and no one suspected that it was even here. Hidden away off Second Street, he had everything a modern Sherlock Holmes needed. He had wanted to show her eventually, but his plans had changed last week. So, he had dug in and worked hard at making his lair as discrete as possible in the old warehouse district of New Brick.

Old waste barrels and graffiti littered these warehouses. Some were his own handiwork, and they gave the place the abandoned feel he needed to carry out his tasks at the warehouse undetected.

He was the law, so what he was doing wasn't wrong. It was so easy, it couldn't be wrong. The purchase of chloroform, GPS equipment, and other sleuth gear for his den were also easy to obtain. It was amazing what one could purchase online. He had things directly shipped to his dad's business, then loaded them in his Jeep, and drove them right down to the warehouse. He hadn't thought twice about it.

No one paid him any attention because, again, he was the law. And being a Tealy put him above the law. He and his family ran this town. These poor, dumb people wouldn't have jobs if it weren't for his father.

He giggled at his cunning. Rori would soon realize just how smart he really was. He had hidden cameras in her condo, GPS on her truck and patrol car. What started out as just his way of keeping her safe had grown into a full operation when Guy had shown up in New Brick. The night that he had watched them wrestling on the floor then falling asleep on her couch had done it.

He faked his disappearance within hours of her betrayal. No way could he go to work and have enough time to prepare his space. No, he had to sacrifice a job that needed his skills for Rori. But it was a small price to pay since he knew that she and Guy wouldn't last.

Dwayne paced the length of what he called the living room as he thought about his love. She needed to see that Guy didn't love her, and only Dwayne could keep her safe. Hell, he was able to bring Guy down in seconds. She deserved better than a weakling like him.

She deserved Dwayne.

Soon, she would be thanking him for his help, and she would tell him that she did love him, had always loved him. His mother had promised that he could have anything he wanted, and he had wanted Rori from day one.

He remembered his first glimpse of her like it was yesterday. He was home on summer vacation after his college graduation. Waltzing into the local Piggly Wiggly, tossing that long ponytail, and instantly he knew...she was perfect for him. He wasted no time introducing himself. Her initial rejection hadn't stopped him from finding out everything about her.

His love for her had grown with every tidbit of information he had acquired. The decision to stay in New Brick, even though he hadn't been here in over six years, had been an easy one. Had he known that his true love was here, he would have fought with his parents to leave boarding school and attend New Brick High. He imagined that he and Rori would have been high school sweethearts, attended prom together, and married right out of college. The whole nine yards—white picket fence, two kids, a dog, and each day she would greet him at the door after a tough day at the office.

As he thought of the lost time with her, he got angry.

The glass he grabbed from the coffee table and threw against the wall shattered. Damn his parents! Instead of loving her and returning his love, Dwayne had lost out on years of happiness.

Why couldn't his parents be normal? Oh, they loved each other, but not in the way he felt about Rori. He would sacrifice everything for her. If his father had felt that way about his mother, then none of this would be happening to him. None of it!

Even though his family had a home here and his father owned half the town, his mother spent much of her time at their homes in New York and Florida. Dwayne had been kicked out of each boarding school he had attended from the time he was eight until eighteen. He didn't understand to this day why his parents had insisted on boarding school. "Can't I just stay with you?" he had asked when he stayed with them for summer break and Christmas.

His mother occasionally visited his various boarding schools but not often. Later, when he was teen, she confessed that she just wasn't fond of children, however, now that he was growing into a perfect young man, she would take the time to guide him.

This guidance from his mother consisted of an "in" to a prestigious college. He barely passed, but that didn't matter. His mother would ensure that he had a first-rate internship with any law firm he wanted.

Too bad that after meeting Rori he hadn't wanted to be a top-notch lawyer anymore. He hadn't wanted anything but her, soaking up every moment in her presence. So, he had informed his mother that the New Brick Police Academy was his career goal. When she hadn't believed him, he had to tell her that he and Rori were secretly in love and she mustn't tell anyone.

It was true—Rori just hadn't realized it yet.

It was sad that it had to take something like this to make her see how much she loved him. All these years he had devoted to loving her, and she had cheated on him with this low-life editor. But Dwayne would forgive her indiscretion. Yes, he would let her make it up to him.

He didn't expect her to be as perfect as him, no one could. His mother had taught him that the Tealy family—and he in particular—were the only family in New Brick worth a damn. Because of his family, this place was on the map.

He stopped his pacing when he realized that he was pulling his hair out again. The pressure of the last week had caused him to do this. It was all Guy Matthews's fault. Dwayne stalked over to a passed-out Guy and slapped him again across the face, just for the fun of it. Worthless excuse of a man.

The alarm on his wristwatch notified him that it was now time for the next phase of his plan. Oh, joy!

He rushed to the closet and started his preparations. The mirror in the closet told him that he would have to tone down his grin.

Not a problem. Dwayne was a master player, and his portrayal of his next act was crucial in winning Rori back.

* * *

Driving her beat today took some effort. Although on the outside Rori appeared her normal coiffed and uniformed self, on the inside she was wilting…from the temperature and from her actions of the past forty-eight hours.

It was her first day back to work, and it was hotter than Hades. And on top of it, she had misgivings about resigning from her job. Last night, she had it all planned out, what she would say, how long of a notice she planned on giving, everything had been decided.

But all she could think about today was regret. Regretting how she had treated her dad and Guy. In fact, she regretted her behavior toward Guy so much that she had already called him.

Twice.

He hadn't picked up either time.

She didn't blame him—she was a witch with a capital *B*. Sure, he hadn't told her that he had been married to that floozy Bambi, but that wasn't the real reason why she was angry.

She was angry at herself for leaving Wyoming the way she

had. In trying to protect Guy from Dwayne, she had brought him right back to Ohio.

And yes, she was angry at herself for being naïve, for believing that she and Guy were some romance written in the stars. That she was his one and only. Hadn't she made the same mistake with Quintin?

If she hadn't found out at that party about vile Quintin, would she have gone on with the relationship?

Probably.

Ugh! It sucked being at work when all she wanted to do was run to Guy and beg forgiveness. The fact that he still wasn't answering his phone told her that his feelings had been hurt by her cruel words.

But they did have to meet tonight for SG business. She would just have to carry on the rest of her day as normal.

Normal, right?

Since she didn't have a patrol partner, Rori was on her own today…which suited her, always the loner. Her route through town was relatively quiet. She had to stop a few skateboarders from skating through Main Street like maniacs, but other than that ruckus and calming down the shop owners, the day had been slow.

Too quiet.

It was just her nerves. She was nervous about the evening with Guy and anxious because he wouldn't pick up the phone and talk to her. Her next stop was the Park and Ride just outside of town. There was usually unwanted activity there, and she felt the need to check there at least twice a day.

Turning in, it was a good thing she had been by because it

seemed an older lady needed her help. A beat-up, tan Buick, late 80's model, had a flat tire. The blue-haired lady trying to change the tire was barely able to lift the jack.

Rori slowed and pulled up behind the car. She stepped out of her vehicle and approached the car. The lady, bent down, seemed to be struggling with something in her purse and the jack at the same time. She must be afraid to leave her purse in the car with all the crime that happened in this area.

"Ma'am, I'm Officer Cross. I'd be happy to help you with your flat."

The old lady rose and grinned. "Thank you, child."

Blue-hair had a wadded-up hankie in her hand and with surprising force, lunged at Rori, covering her face. Chilling laughter rang out, and Rori struggled in vain as she realized that the little old lady in disguise was Dwayne Tealy…

Rori felt a tug on her hands, then heard a whisper.

"Rori, wake up, sweetheart."

Finally raising her head from an odd angle, she tried to assess the situation.

"Where am I?" She must have murmured too loudly because Guy shushed her. She knew that voice anywhere, and only one man in her entire life had ever called her sweetheart.

Her heart swelled with love, and she almost cried out to him but stopped herself as he whispered that Dwayne had indeed gone crazy and had abducted him yesterday right in front of the range.

They were underground somewhere and tied back-to-back in old, metal chairs. The kind you would find in an old warehouse. Immediately, she knew where they were. Dwayne was cunning, she would give him that. No one, and she knew *no one*, would think to look here.

Dwayne enjoyed the finer things in life, and nobody was going to believe that he had chosen a hideout in an old, dingy, abandoned warehouse.

Reaching back, she touched Guy's hands with hers, letting him know that she understood. She was too afraid to talk, afraid that her voice would carry, afraid that she would let her feelings show. Now was not the time to be scared.

Guy spoke quietly. "I've been pretending to be out of it when I hear Dwayne approaching. He is confident that he is the better man and I'm a weakling." She could almost imagine the smirk on Guy's face as he said, "Dwayne may be cunning enough to have concocted this plan and gotten us down here, but it won't work."

Trusting that her voice wouldn't rise to a yell, she asked, "Why?"

"Because I've almost got my hands untied, and he hasn't got a clue." To emphasize, he grabbed one of her hands and gave it a quick squeeze.

"Guy, I—"

"I think I hear something."

Sure enough, Dwayne had returned to his den. She could hear his chilling laughter. She felt Guy go limp and assumed that he was playing the weakling role again. She tried to do the same.

Rori felt eyes on her, and she must have stiffened, drawing Dwayne's attention to her. "Rori, my love, you can't fool me. I know you are awake. Let me show you how smart I really am. You will be so proud."

She gave up the ruse and looked up at him. How had the weasel, the thorn in her side, become such a nut job? Still wearing the old lady disguise, but his lipstick and wig were jacked up. No telling what he would do—he had lost what few marbles he had in that brain of his.

She shook her head to clear the last of the cobwebs. *Think, think!* Guy was untied and alert. Everything was going to be fine. Plus, she should have returned her patrol car hours ago. Someone would be out looking for her. Right?

Unfortunately, Dwayne had thought to remove all her weapons. So, there wasn't anything Guy could take from her to assist him. Still, they had the advantage. Dwayne was running out of time and he surely knew that.

He cut the rope across her chest and hauled her to her feet. Her hands were still bound behind her back, so she couldn't stop his offending hands roaming over her body.

Filled with disgust, she did what any tied-up girl would do— she spit in his face and kicked his shins. "Get your slimy hands off of me!"

Unbelievably, Dwayne's face changed into that of a madman. "Mother said I could have any woman I wanted, and you, my pet, I have always wanted. Tell me you love me. Show me how much you love me."

Guy chose that moment to jump to her rescue, knocking

over the metal chairs and running toward Dwayne. Dwayne aimed his gun at her and started to pull the trigger.

Rori yelled, "No!" at the same time she heard a shout by the stairs leading into the basement.

It happened so fast, she couldn't move Guy out of her way. She was wearing her vest, for crying out loud. She fell with his weight on top of her at the same time Dwayne dropped by her feet.

"Aurora?"

The other shout had been her father, and he was leaning across her, checking Guy's pulse. From the grim look on his face, Guy wasn't in good shape as he lay motionless on top of her.

Soon, most of the NBPD were in the basement, administering CPR to Guy and cuffing a sobbing, belligerent Dwayne. Edward had shot Dwayne in the arm and the leg.

"She loves me. Tell them, Rori, tell them all how much you love me! Mother said you were to be mine. She promised, she promised!" His screams kept getting louder.

She heard crying and realized that the agonizing pain in her chest was the result of her tears. She had finally broken that wall and was crying like a baby as they wheeled Guy to the ambulance. Her father walked with her and hugged her. "Everything will be alright. That boy is a strong one."

Sniffling, she hugged her dad and cried harder. She cried for Guy taking a bullet for her, she cried for not telling him yesterday that she loved him, she cried for her mom and grieved for the times she had wanted to cry and hadn't.

In between tears, she found the courage to tell her father, "I'm sorry for yesterday. I want you to be happy."

Edward just held her tighter, and said, "I'm sorry too, so hush now. It will be alright, all is forgiven."

She cried until they reached the hospital. She and her dad sat in the waiting room as her co-workers asked her about Dwayne. She answered their questions and asked some of her own. How did the NBPD find her? How was Guy? What happened to Dwayne?

Her father had taken a page out of Dwayne's book and had implanted a tracker in her boots. A quick glance at her father, and he just nodded. "So, how did you know I would be wearing this pair?"

"I didn't. I put trackers in every pair of shoes you owned while you were in Wyoming and I snuck back into your condo and did your others while you were asleep last night."

She should have been appalled that she slept so soundly, but instead she was grateful. Grateful that her father was sneaky. "Thanks, Dad."

The emotional scene was broken up as an emergency room doctor entered and asked, "Guy Matthews's family?"

Rori rushed forward. "He is my boyfriend." It was the first time she had spoken those words aloud. They felt right.

"I'm sorry, miss, but family only." The doctor began to turn away.

The NBPD chief stepped forward, "Listen, the man took a bullet for her, tell her how he is doing."

The elderly doctor smiled. "Alright. Mr. Matthews has lost a lot of blood, but he is stable. The bullet went straight through his right shoulder. He will be able to see visitors in a couple hours."

Rori raised her head. "Thank you, God." Never again would she take love for granted. They had been given a second chance, and she decided to act on it. "Dad, will you wait with me until it is time? I don't want to be here alone."

"Sure, princess," he said as he sat down and held out his arm to curl around her shoulder.

Princess? Her dad had never called her that before, but she liked it, she thought, as she snuggled into her dad's embrace to wait out the next few hours.

# CHAPTER FOURTEEN

G uy heard crying and opened his eyes. His head swam, so he closed them again. What had happened? The last thing he remembered was slipping into darkness.

He tried opening his eyes once more. This time he could bear the dizziness. If the sterile white room didn't tell him he was in a hospital bed, the IV in his arm gave it away.

The crying continued as he tried to move his hands to alert someone that he was awake, but his hand was immobile due to the iron grip someone had on it.

Rori. His Rori.

She was an angel, crying over his bed. He had never heard her cry, and yet here she was…soaking his hospital gown.

He hated hospitals, and his shoulder hurt like hell, but he and Rori were together, and that was all that mattered. He tried to raise his hand to rub her hair away from her cheek. "Damn," he managed to croak out between parched lips.

"Guy!" Kisses rained down on his face. "I'm sorry, I'm sorry. I love you. I left Wyoming so you wouldn't get hurt, and you show up here and get hurt. I never meant for you to get hurt." This didn't sound like his girl, finally admitting how she felt. It almost made getting shot worth it.

Gorgeous Rori, a bit ruffled with dark circles under her eyes. She looked perfect to his medicine-clouded mind, and he didn't even care that her words of love had turned into nagging.

"Guy Matthews. You fool of a man, why did you step in front of me? I was wearing my vest. Of all the dumb things to do!"

Now, that was his Rori.

"Hi to you too." His voice was still a bit hoarse. He winced as he tried to move into a more comfortable position. His shoulder burned. That couldn't be good.

"Crap, I'm going to yell for your nurse. They should know you are awake anyhow." She rushed from the room before he could tell her that he was fine.

His nurse, Helga, muscled her way into the small room like a linebacker, checked his chart, and administered his pain medicine. With a stern look at Rori, she said, "Visiting hours are soon going to be over."

He had just woken and wasn't ready to let her go yet. "Wait, Rori."

Expectant eyes looked at him. Her tears had dried, but her eyes and nose were red from all the crying she had done. Still in her uniform, wrinkled, and again with a messy ponytail, much like how she looked at the range last night. Although he preferred a crying Rori to a pissed-off Rori firing a Smith & Wesson any day of the week.

Man, how he loved this woman. "Come here."

With a quickness that he could appreciate, she was soon at his side kissing him deeply. A cough reminded them of Nurse Helga's presence.

"I will see you first thing in the morning, Mr. Editor."

"Is that a promise or a threat?"

"Both." Then leaning down, she whispered that Helga would give him a sponge bath if he didn't rest and eat his vegetables.

\* \* \*

Rori rushed through her morning routine to get to the hospital. She couldn't believe that she had overslept. Good thing she was organized and had her uniforms ready, and all her gear easily accessible. Today of all days was not the day to be running late. She had promised Guy that she would be there. She wanted to be the first person he saw when he woke up.

For the rest of their lives, she was going to be right beside him. How would he feel if she proposed to him? Knowing Guy the way she did, he would probably be offended and would want to satisfy her romantic dreams of a movie-scene proposal. She would let him take the lead, something that she had never let a man do before. Yes, she did indeed love Guy Matthews.

Rori Matthews.

That thought brought a smile to her face. My, oh my, being in love felt strange. Tight knots in her stomach, not sure why she felt dizzy. She was head over heels and all the other corny phrases she had ever heard in her life.

Opening the hospital room door, she was shocked to see that he wasn't in the bed. It was clean and freshly made. She touched the sheets. Cold.

Running out of the room, she stopped at the nurse's station. "Where is Mr. Matthews?"

"Miss, calm down. There were some complications, but—"

Almost reaching over the counter, Rori rounded on the tiny blond nurse and said through clenched teeth, "Tell me where he is."

"I can't do that. Mr. Matthews's family came in, and he has been moved to the private wing of the hospital."

"What family? His parents are in California, and he barely sees them."

"Yes, both Dr. Matthewses made it in late last night. Unfortunately, I can't tell you more than that."

"Well, will you put a call through to his room? I know he would like to see me."

"Certainly, hold just a moment." The nurse handed her the phone.

Rori tapped her fingers on the counter as she waited for him to answer the phone.

A woman answered, which startled her. "Umm, yes, this is Rori Cross calling for Guy." Assuming the stern voice on the other end was Nurse Helga, strange, she didn't think nurses answered the phone for patients, but maybe the private wing ran things differently.

The stern voice rose an octave or two. "Miss Cross. This is

Guy's mother, Dr. Matthews. I'm afraid your visit today is unwanted. Please leave my son alone." And the call was disconnected.

The tiny nurse frowned as if she had known, and probably did, what kind of reception Rori would receive. Still, not wanting to accept defeat, she lied and said, "Mr. Matthews is sleeping, they told me to come back later today." Then paused as if she remembered something, "Oh, they forgot to tell me which room number."

Being a cop had its perks, and one of them was the ability to bluff. The nurse fell for her subterfuge, and the room number easily tumbled from her lips.

"Thank you," Rori said calmly, as to not draw attention to herself. Then she marched straight up to room 305 and was met with one of her co-workers in uniform standing guard outside of Guy's room. Thank goodness it was Henry—she could manage Henry. He was one of the few on the force that she would actually call a friend, the only one who had ever stood up to Dwayne in her defense. Still, she wasn't going to go easy on him when it came to getting in through the door to see Guy.

"Henry, what the heck are you doing here?"

He looked around, almost afraid, then in a hushed whisper said, "Rori, you aren't supposed to be here. Get out of here."

Hands on hips, she felt that for the first time in her life she might throw a fit that even Bri Walker would admire. "Henry. I'm going through that door. Not you, not Guy's mother, not even that scary nurse is going to stop me."

She pushed Henry out of the way, knowing that he wouldn't dare lay a hand on her. Opening the door, her eyes darted immediately to the hospital bed for Guy. The paleness of his skin scared her. What the heck happened to the happy, recovering man she had seen last night?

Moving more into the room, she was met with two cold stares. The Doctors Matthews were an impressive couple. An intimidating couple. Guy's father dressed in an understated fashion in a tan blazer, designer jeans, and loafers. His mother, on the other hand, screamed fashionista. Her multi-colored wrap dress looked like something Salma Hayek would wear, and her high heel wedges and excessive jewelry should've looked tacky but didn't.

Yes, overall, the two made quite an impression. And for the first time in a long time, Rori felt intimidated.

"You must be Rori." This came from Guy's father. "I'm Doctor Gerald Matthews. My wife, Doctor Margaret Matthews."

Margaret Matthews just glared at her. Okay, minus one member in the Rori fan club. There were worse things than having Guy's mother hate her, right?

The next few minutes confirmed she was wrong.

His mother stepped forward and slapped her. Her husband grabbed at his wife's hand, but it was too late. Under her breath, so she wouldn't wake Guy, she said, "Get out. You almost killed my son."

"Margaret. That is enough." Then turning to Rori, Gerald said, "Miss Cross, I will walk you to the door."

Outside in the private hallway, she and Henry listened to Gerald's recitation of what Guy had been through during the night.

"Miss Cross, I'm sorry about my wife. You have to understand what a roller coaster ride this has been for us. We had no idea Guy was even in Ohio, then to get a call from Brock that something had happened."

"Brock?"

"Yes, Brock Walker."

"I've met Brock, Dr. Matthews. What does he have to do with this?"

"Well, Brock is Guy's emergency contact, not us. Not his parents. It makes sense. They live in the same state and have grown up like brothers. But when he called and said something had happened to Guy in Ohio, we just lost it. Regret, worry, anger. All these emotions rolling over us on our trip here."

She still didn't understand why Brock hadn't made it to Guy's bedside. "Why didn't Brock make it? Why call you if he is the contact Guy wanted?"

"Because Brock injured himself on the job a couple days ago and is unable to fly."

"I understand that you both would be upset that Guy took a bullet for me, and I have ripped him over and over for doing so, but something doesn't add up. When I left Guy last night, he was fine. He was smiling and sure, he was in pain, but he didn't look like he does now."

Gerald Matthews grimaced. "When we arrived last night, Guy hadn't been attended to in several hours, infection had set in, and he had an extremely high fever. The hospital had been in an uproar over a three-car-crash, and they were overwhelmed. Guy suffered because of the lack of staff on duty. Apparently, there have been massive layoffs, and there is still some restructuring going on."

She gasped, and tears welled up as she thought about Guy being alone in a room, unable to ask for help. "I should have insisted on staying, but the night nurse made me leave."

Guy got his compassion and tender heart from his father, she thought as Gerald Matthews grabbed her in a bear hug. "He will be fine once the infection is cleared and his fever is down. Margaret is having regrets right now, and she is taking it out on you. Not being part of Guy's life and then almost losing him last night, well, you can imagine that she isn't her usual calm self."

She hugged him back. "Thanks, I understand."

"Come back in the morning. I'm sure things will be brighter then."

"I will." She said it with her head down so Gerald, and an eavesdropping Henry, wouldn't see the tears she was trying to hold back.

It seemed that since she let the dam break yesterday, she had done nothing *but* cry. She wasn't a therapist, but all her years of trying to be tough to earn her father's respect and then not grieving over her mom's passing had taken its toll.

She was officially a basket case. Yep, one of those emotional women whose dreams depended on a man. But he was a heck of man to have a dream pinned to.

A slight cough reminded her that she was standing in the hall of the private wing of the hospital.

Henry.

Apparently, Gerald had gone back into Guy's room, and she hadn't even noticed.

"Go home, Cross. Get some sleep. I'll call the chief and tell him I sent you home." He touched her arm in comfort. Man, these tears really worked on men. Too bad she hadn't learned that trick years ago, not that she would have turned on the tears to get her way, but it would've helped her better understand relationships.

"Thanks, Henry. See you tomorrow." With that, she planned to go home and call Bri. Her promised phone call was long overdue.

The short ride back to her condo consisted of blaring the latest tunes on the radio. Music always fed her soul, and her soul needed nourishment. Pulling into her lot, she noticed someone at her door.

Not just someone—Brianne!

Jumping out of her truck, Rori rushed to the door. "Bri! Thank goodness you're here!"

In her usual snippy, bite-me attitude, Bri said, "Of course I'm here! Brock had to get himself hurt like a dumbass, and one of us had to be here for Guy and for you."

In true Bri form, she was wearing lots of leather, high-heeled boots, and very short shorts. "Are you gonna let me in or what? It's freaking humid out here. Some of these clothes have to go!"

Rori giggled. Yes, giggled. "Of course. You can borrow some of my shorts and tanks." Unlocking her door, she filled Bri in on Guy's condition, and the request of his father to come tomorrow morning for a visit.

Bri took a quick look around the condo. "Honey, you are so vanilla. Just look at this place. Beige, tan, and white. And I *do* own comfy clothes, ya know."

She dropped her bag right on the foyer floor. "Where do you want me?"

Rori laughed. She had missed her new friend and felt that having her here was exactly what she needed now. "I don't have a spare room, but you can take my room. I will take the couch."

"Of course, you don't have a spare room. You have it filled with clothes and shoes. Am I right?"

She led Bri to the "spare room" and laughed as her friend sounded shocked. "I knew it! You and I have more things in common than I realized. This is exactly what my spare room looks like."

And Bri began to question her on her bullet re-loading methods, her targets, and anything else that caught her eye in the room. "Let's go practice and blow off some steam."

Rori was up for that. It was good to finally have a friend to go on spa days but to also be able to go to the range with.

Things were looking up.

# CHAPTER FIFTEEN

Bri and Rori enjoyed the evening. Forgetting about the chaos with Guy's mom, both were relieved that his doctor parents were present to help him on the road to recovery. Bri filled her in on some childhood memories, and she had finally stopped the urge to cry every five seconds, and instead laughter filled her small condo.

The night at the range had been a good break for both of them, and for the first time in days, she felt hopeful. She was hopeful that Guy would recover, hopeful that they would have a life together, and hopeful that she and her dad were on the right path.

Although Brianne hadn't mentioned Tucker, Rori knew that something major had happened between the two of them. She knew that Bri cared about him but wasn't willing to question her about it when she had thoroughly messed up her own love life as of late.

Tomorrow morning would bring answers about Guy's condition and his mother's anger toward Rori. She could only trust that Bri and Tucker would figure it all out. Not wait till it was almost too late to decide what they both wanted out of their relationship.

Ugh. She wanted to step in and say something to her friend but she was too raw. She had just stopped crying a couple hours ago and didn't want to start up the waterworks again. This sensitive stuff sucked.

After a pig-out on pizza and chips, both were ready to hit the hay. Rori gave Brianne her room and camped out on the couch with a new book. She didn't think she would sleep after all that happened but soon wasn't able to keep her eyes focused on the words. Giving up, she used her bookmark to hold her place and gave in to the weariness she felt.

The reprieve didn't last. Rori woke after a terrible nightmare. Last night played like a movie in slow motion, Guy getting shot, her father shooting Dwayne…all of it came back with a fierceness that had her sitting up on the edge of the couch, gasping for air.

She'd had nightmares after her mom had passed, but nothing like this—watching Guy jump in front of her, then the bullet knocking him down, then falling. She had thought he was dead and that her world had ended.

What a week this had been. When had her life turned into a Lifetime movie? Seriously, if she was the heroine, she needed to act like one. It was time for her to get her mojo back.

Checking the clock, it was four a.m. Too early for the hospital, but not too early for an old western marathon and cold pizza.

Halfway into the movie, she heard, "What the hell, Rori!" Turning, she spotted Bri in a polka-dotted nightie, sleep mask pushed up on her head, and her hair shooting out around her head like a lioness on fire. Evidently Bri was *not* a morning person.

"Sorry, did I wake you?"

"You have got to be kidding me. Did you wake me? Of course you did, or I wouldn't be standing here yelling at you for waking me up." Bri rubbed her eyes and stared at Rori. "Is there any more cold pizza?"

The redhead grabbed a couple pieces, got herself a glass of water, and proceeded to watch the movie with Rori. They didn't say another word, as if Bri could see the unease in her eyes and left it alone.

And Rori let her. They pretended that it was normal to be up at four a.m., eating cold pizza and watching old westerns. Typical for a pair of twenty-somethings.

One thing she could appreciate—if Guy never forgave her for not trusting him—was that her time with him brought Brianne into her life. She had the feeling that she and Bri would be forever friends. The kind that had each other's backs, no matter the consequences.

She realized that the movie had finished, and Brianne was still silent. Looking over, she saw that Bri had fallen asleep again, her hair still shooting out all over. There was such a fierceness and sadness to her. Rori hoped one day Bri would confide in her, let her know what troubled her, what made her do the things she did, what made her push Tucker away when he was so obviously in love with her. At the concert, he'd carried her out of there as if his life depended on it.

Glancing at her watch, she saw that it was now six a.m., time to get ready and make it to the station and see what had happened to Dwayne. Rori had her thoughts on Dwayne's breakdown, thinking that the scene at the Pizza Grill had pushed him over the edge. What possessed her to pour that beer over his head? Because of her, Guy lay in a hospital bed fighting off an infection that could have killed him.

His mother was right...it was all her fault.

But this just made her more determined to make things right. And after her stop at the station, she was headed to the hospital.

Showered, dressed, and headed out the door, she looked at her friend still asleep on the couch and decided to leave her a quick note. Bri had her cell number and could call if she woke up soon also.

Now that Rori had a purpose for her day, she was raring to go and was tucking in the blue shirt to her uniform when she was stopped by Henry waiting for her at the station. "Cross, I'm surprised to see you here so early."

"Yeah, well. I have two people to check on today. What's the news?" Henry knew she meant Dwayne.

"Well, they pulled in the NBPD shrink, and Dwayne has something called a narcissistic personality disorder. If you ask me, he got it from his mama."

She had always known something was off with Dwayne Tealy. "Tell me what this disorder is...does this mean he doesn't have to do time?"

"No, he will do time. The shrink said Dwayne had a feeling

of being god-like. He is self-centered and was spoiled by his mother. When he couldn't have you, he flipped the switch."

They all knew his characteristics, but she still felt awful that she was the cause of this entire mess. "Can he be cured?"

"No, it isn't treatable with medicine. He will probably stay locked up for a good long while. Shrink also says it is only a matter of time before he hurts someone again. He has been in the room pulling his hair out. Talking about his mother, very deep issues there."

This was deep, even for Dwayne.

Henry was on a roll and wanted to give her every detail. "Apparently, Mr. Tealy isn't even his real father. Dwayne never knew, but that is why Mr. Tealy sent him to boarding schools all over the U.S. He didn't want the reminder of his wife's infidelity."

Wow. Her life was indeed a movie script. "Thanks, Henry. Since I don't start my shift for a couple more hours, do you mind if I head out? I have somewhere I need to be."

"Sure, Cross. Tell Guy hey and we are all pulling for him."

Guy awoke to his mother and Rori speaking quietly. He had to strain to hear them. He hurt all over, so his concentration wasn't one hundred percent.

In his entire life, he had never heard his mother speak so earnestly before. In fact, he was surprised that his mother was here at all since Brock had been listed as his emergency contact for as long as he could remember.

He tried to tune into the conversation and overheard his mother say, "I'm sorry for slapping you yesterday, truly sorry. Please forgive me."

Slapping? His mother slapped Rori?

When had this slap occurred? The last he remembered after being shot was seeing Rori after his surgery. Visiting hours ended and she had to go, but that was the last he recalled.

Everything after her visit was a bit of a blur.

"What happened?" He didn't realize he had spoken the question aloud until both his mother and Rori gasped.

They were at his side in a split second, one on each side, that was. He reached out and grabbed Rori's hand. "What happened?"

He didn't think his mother would mind his preference to Rori seeing as how he had only seen her twice a year since he was eighteen. Her career had always come before her family.

Rori hesitated, and he saw tears in her eyes. She was crying again. She didn't answer and instead allowed his doctor mother to explain what had happened to him during the last twenty-four hours.

The door to his hospital room slowly opened, and his father walked in. Damn, his dad looked like he hadn't slept in days. Gerald Matthews assessed the situation, and upon seeing Guy awake, Rori in tears, and his mother hovering by his side, Gerald said, "Margaret, let's go to the cafeteria and compare the food to our hospital."

Surprisingly, she didn't argue, but instead bent down, kissed his cheek, and squeezed his hand.

It seemed his almost deadly accident had brought out the

nurturing side of his mother. Guy couldn't remember the last time his mother had even hugged him, let alone kissed him. She had always been a cool, business-like mother. While his dad had made more of an effort these last few years, Margaret Matthews had remained solidly cold.

After college, when he had married Bambi, it had been to get a rise out of his mother. That hadn't even worked. She had just stopped speaking to him until the divorce had been finalized. Then she pretended he hadn't even married someone not of her choosing.

But his dad had called him and still reached out to him. He remembered one phone call from his dad. "Son, I have never told you what to do, but just remember you must also be married to your best friend or it will never work. When instant attraction dies, you must have something in common. Take it from me."

After witnessing the calming influence his father had over his mother, he knew then what he had never realized before. His parents were friends. They had something in common. Their shared goal of healing the sick.

He and Rori were friends, and outside of Brock, she was probably his best friend. Around her, he had been goofy and carefree. He had never dared to be "normal" around any girl he found attractive.

But with her it was different.

It was special…it was *real*.

"Rori? What are you doing way over there? Come here," he said with a little more oomph than he had intended.

She bristled at his tone. "Just because it is my fault you're lying there doesn't give you the right to go bossing me, Mr. Matthews."

More softly this time, he raised his arm to motion her toward him and winced.

She rushed to him then. "You stupid man. Stop hurting yourself."

Smiling, he said, "I'm not hurting any longer. You are here now. Rori, there is something I want to ask you—"

The door opened, and Edward Cross stepped in. "Rori, Guy. Don't mean to barge in, but I wanted to check on the two of you and give you some news."

They looked at him expectantly. "What is it, Dad?" Edward was not his usual pristine self. Wrinkled shirt and jeans and missing a few pens from his pocket protector.

"I'm getting married to Miss Stanwick…tomorrow."

"What?" Rori yelped a little and must have realized how it sounded. "That's great, Dad, but why so suddenly?"

"Well, seeing as how life is so short and you just never know. So, the wedding will be Friday evening, six o'clock at the farm. Hope you both can make it."

With his normal briskness, he turned and left the hospital room.

"Damn," Guy whispered under his breath. All romantic thoughts he had for tonight were over. Rori would probably be too wrapped up in her father's wedding. She surprised him, by pushing him over on the bed.

"Mr. Matthews. I need a date for Friday night, so no sudden movements for you, I need you out of here because I will not be going to my father's wedding alone." She put her head on his good shoulder, and even though her gun and holster were digging him in his thigh, he shut up and put his good arm around her.

"Whatever you say, sweetheart." After that, he was too tired to hold his eyes open any longer or mention his plans for the future.

When he woke again, Rori was gone, and his parents were sitting in the drab olive-green chairs in his hospital room.

"Where's Rori?" he grumbled, not happy that again she had gone before he had a chance to ask her what had been on his mind and talk to her about the night Dwayne had taken him. He had wanted to pour his heart out to her, get everything off his chest. From not telling her about his ex and waking up in that hell-hole basement, to her crying over him the hospital room.

So much of the last week was playing through his mind like a bad movie.

His father answered. "She went to work, then planned on helping her father's fiancé, and said to tell you she would be back as soon as she could."

Margaret interjected, "The doctors said that you could be released Friday morning as long as there isn't any sign of the infection still lingering."

"Well, that is great news." He perked up, but why did he have the sinking suspicion that his mother hadn't given him all the information?

"Mom. What is it?"

"Well, you still have a slight fever. So, the quickest way for you to be rid of the infection is—"

"No. I won't do it!"

"Now, Guy, it is only a small needle, and that was a long time ago. I can't believe you still have such a phobia about getting a little shot."

As soon as his mother finished her sentence, the nurse came in, and he believed her name was Helga. She had arms like a linebacker. "Roll over," she commanded. Fearing Helga's wrath more than the needle she held, Guy did the only thing he could...he rolled over.

# CHAPTER SIXTEEN

Small lights twinkled and hung whimsically in the trees. A dozen white chairs lined up before the arbor in the Cross backyard. Pink flowers from every greenhouse in New Brick lined the walk in various pots. Some matched, some didn't it, but the farm looked stunning. And it should since Rori, Bri, and Elizabeth Stanwick had all worked most of the previous night and early this morning. The small ceremony would be picturesque.

Inhaling and exhaling, Rori rolled her shoulders to loosen them. A party planner she wasn't. Bri, on the other hand, enjoyed all the pre-party planning, and she and "Bethie," as her father called Elizabeth, were close to being chummy.

If she admitted it to herself, she did enjoy Elizabeth's company as well, but she *refused* to call her Bethie. She had switched from Miss Stanwick to Elizabeth sometime during the day.

No matter.

Tonight, her father would get married, and Guy would be released from the hospital just in time. She had stopped by to visit him last night after the decorating marathon, but he was out cold.

His parents were still there, and she had invited them to the wedding. They both seemed pleased as punch and had agreed to come. She really liked Gerald and she thought she could grow to like Margaret. She may not have been the best mother to Guy as a child, but she was using this second chance that had been thrown at her for the best.

It seemed that all drama was wrapping up quite nicely, even on the Dwayne front. Mrs. Tealy had thrown such an awesome fit at the police station that she was restrained and then detained. Her husband had arrived with lawyers, and soon Mrs. Tealy was escorted out of the station.

Rori had it on good authority that Jeanette Tealy would be ensconced in a private facility, which Rori liked to refer to as the loony bin. Poor Dwayne wouldn't get off as easily, since his condition was diagnosed by the shrink. He was fit to stand trial, and it seemed that Mr. Tealy was not going to throw his weight around to get Dwayne out of this one.

Even though things were calming down in Ohio, Rori missed her time in Wyoming with Guy. She hoped to get back there soon. Her heart yearned for the beauty of Wyoming, and the laid-back lifestyle she had a glimpse of when she stayed with Guy.

A thought occurred to her. She had yet to prove to Guy just how deep her feelings ran for him. She believed actions spoke louder than words, and an idea popped into her head suddenly. Checking her leather wristwatch, she found that she had a few hours before the ceremony. Perfect. Just enough time to get to the station, go home, and do what she needed to do, and then get back before Guy and his parents arrived.

It took an hour to convince the chief that she was resigning and planned on placing a formal resignation letter in his hands tomorrow. With her path forward in place, Rori immediately felt better.

Next, she stopped at her local department store, got the needed supplies, and headed back home. She took an hour and did as much as she could before getting ready for the wedding.

*This will have to do*, she thought.

Unfortunately, Elizabeth Stanwick requested that Rori be her one and only bridesmaid. The pink cotton sundress Elizabeth had picked out for her suited her, and it was something that she would have chosen herself. So, the first time she laid eyes on Guy since her last visit to the hospital happened while walking down the aisle.

A current went through her as she met his eyes. Did he feel it too?

His color was healthier, and even with his arm in a sling, he looked good enough to eat. White button-up shirt, khakis, and flip-flops. Probably so he wouldn't have to tie his shoes himself, she thought. As she walked by his row, he gave her a wide smile.

His parents sat on either side of him. They too grinned. For the first time, she realized how much he resembled his parents.

It had never occurred to her since she had never seen the Drs. Matthews smile or appear happy.

She passed their row and looked ahead to where her father stood awaiting his bride. Never in a million years had she imagined this scene. He appeared so happy, and she let it go. The fear, the guilt, all those destructive emotions that she had bottled up toward her father. She wanted him to be happy, in his marriage and in his new life.

She stepped to the side, hesitated, then walked to her father and pecked him on the cheek quickly, then stepped back. That small action spoke volumes. In front of all their guests, with just a small kiss, Rori had given her blessing to her father and Elizabeth.

The ceremony was breathtaking, and there weren't too many dry eyes in attendance.

The small reception took place on the Cross's back deck. Simple fare and good company.

Rori walked over to where Guy sat on a deck lounger. "Want to take a short walk with me?"

He rose slowly. "Sure, sweetheart."

She grabbed his hand and matched her usually quick stride with his slower one. She led him down a slightly overgrown path, talking all the way. "So, I hope you are up to this, but I wanted to get you alone to talk a bit."

"Sweetheart, you never have to apologize for wanting to get me alone." He gripped her hand like a lifeline.

Rori gave his fingers a quick squeeze and released him before she used both hands to push through some bushes. They entered an open meadow. The large quilt and picnic basket she had set out an hour earlier sat beside the small pond.

"What is all this, Rori?" he said in awe of the view and the romantic scene she had created.

He took her hand this time and strode to the quilt. "I'm wondering what a girl who claimed she couldn't cook would put in a picnic basket."

They sat close together, and she began to pull fresh fruit, cheese, and spring water from one side of the basket.

"Just a little something I threw together. As I said earlier, I wanted to be alone. I didn't want to wait any longer."

He leaned forward and kissed her softly. "I didn't want to wait any longer to kiss you."

She couldn't wait any longer either. She had him right where she wanted him. "Guy, I brought you out here because I'm ready. I love you more than words can express, and I want us to be together forever."

"Rori, you had me from the first swish of your long, blond ponytail. I saw you standing there, and something just shot straight through my heart. Marry me?"

He reached into his pocket and produced a black ring box. He opened it to reveal an exquisite princess-cut diamond ring.

"I love it." She couldn't believe the feeling as he pushed the ring on the appropriate finger.

He laughed. "Since you aren't disagreeing, I assume the answer is yes."

"Yes!" She pulled him to her and showed him what she couldn't express in words.

# EPILOGUE

**H**oneymoons *were awesome,* Rori thought as she lounged on the lanai, soaking up the warm Kauai sun. She could stay in Kauai forever. She loved the tropical paradise, even the rainfall each day. Most importantly, she loved that she and Guy had finally married.

They had planned on eloping, but his mother had offered to plan a huge wedding. Rori had enjoyed her company and the elaborate wedding details. She hated the fact it had taken six months to plan, but the results were memorable.

They had been on their honeymoon for almost two weeks, and she still couldn't believe her good fortune.

"Sweetheart, I have a surprise for you."

He was such a hopeless romantic. He strode through the small sitting area of their suite to reach her outside. She made room for him on the lounger, and he placed a manila folder on her lap.

"What have you done now, Mr. Matthews?"

Hesitantly, she opened the folder and pulled out several papers. "House plans?"

"Yes, and not just any house plans. This is for our second house in Ohio. I bought the property adjacent to your father's farm."

Overwhelmed with emotion, she didn't know what to say. Not only did she have her dream career traveling around the country, she shared Guy's exquisite lodge in Wyoming, and would now have a place next to her father. It was too much.

"Say something, sweetheart."

She looked up into his smiling face, and instead of thanking him, she said, "I think this house plan needs a few more bedrooms for future little Matthewses, don't you?"

# ABOUT THE AUTHOR

Maren lives on twelve acres with her husband and dog. She enjoys taking walks, traveling, writing and reading. You can learn more about Maren and her upcoming projects by visiting www.MarenBirk.com.